Easier
Than It Seems

Bob Bennett

Clink
Street

London | New York

Published by Clink Street Publishing 2020

Copyright © 2020

First edition.

ISBN: 978-1-913568-59-7 – paperback
978-1-913568-60-3 – ebook

Chapter One

Ken Blake had left Eastfield Secondary Modern in 1941 aged fifteen. World War II was well into its full fury. Just days before his fifteenth birthday, German bombers were again blitzing London and many landmark buildings had been badly damaged. Even churches were not spared. The Battle of Britain was barely over and now the country had The Blitz to contend with. The RAF continued to do its part bombing aircraft factories in Bremen and other installations crucial to the German war machine. But the Luftwaffe were similarly focussed with British ports suffering badly. Industrial centres were also being pounded by German bombs night after night. Raids on Coventry and Birmingham were getting too close for comfort. Ken, together with his father Albert, his mother Mabel, his younger brother and sister were obliged to sleep in the Anderson Shelter buried at the bottom of the garden. On Ken's sixteenth birthday it was announced on the BBC Home Service that Hitler had met with Mussolini at Berchtesgaden. Seems they'd agreed that Hitler would provide aid to North Africa. He didn't know it at the time, but young Ken too would be in North Africa before his next birthday.

At Eastfield Secondary Modern Ken had been a member of the Combined Cadet Force and fit and able as he was, he was conscripted into his father's old regiment the Seaforth Highlanders and mobilised. Initially he was posted to the Regimental Headquarters, Fort George, in the north of Scotland for basic training.

Leicester London Road railway station was heaving with a mass of humanity searching for friends, relatives, lost luggage, the right platform, the toilets, who knew what. Ken followed a group of blokes in khaki on the assumption that they knew where they were going. They did. It appeared that the entire male population of Leicestershire between the ages of sixteen and twenty were boarding the LMS train on platform two. The train was crammed with young men, boys really, being transported to their respective posts. Just occasionally Ken recognised one or two chaps as his old schoolfriends. They appeared to be just as apprehensive as he was. But there was always one 'Jack the lad' – or in this case 'Jock the lad'.

Also, an old boy from Eastfield, as large as life and cocksure as ever, there in the corridor was Duncan McClean, never known by any name other than Jock for reasons his given name might suggest! Ken knew Jock. They'd been in the same class at school and now they were both on their way to war via Scotland. What could be worse?

Jock, 'small but perfectly formed' as he liked to describe himself, drew himself up to his full five foot and two inches and gave Ken a mock salute. Despite his diminutive height Jock always cut a dash. He always looked sharp, what with his Brylcreemed hair and even at sixteen years old a pencil-line moustache he had the features of a young Clark Gable the movie star, and a self-assured demeanour. All the girls fancied Jock and didn't he know it. Not that he would ever admit it, Ken was just a bit envious.

Not that they'd been school pals as such, in fact the opposite if anything, their time at Fort George threw them together and for practical purposes they became mates of a sort. With fourteen weeks of basic training completed they were both shipped off to North Africa. But not to join the infantry at Tobruk which had been widely rumoured as their destination. No, the Highland regiments shipped to Accra the capital of the Gold Coast and on to Western Ashanti. The fall of France and the entry of Italy into the war made June 1940 something of a turning point, not just in the Mediterranean but also in West Africa. The Gold Coast, surrounded by French colonies as it was had been relying on their support but now their alliance had become tantamount to a neutrality as the Colonial French ignored De Gaulle's call to fight on. Therefore, they were liable to be leant on by Germany. This would have caused disruption to the British Colonies. Ken's regiment hosted Allied aircraft and played an important role in assisting the Colonial troops in taking control of Italian East Africa. At the same time the regiment assisted in the rebuilding of the infrastructure of the country, badly damaged after an earthquake in 1939. By comparison to their compatriots in the Desert Rats and in the other theatres of war both in Africa and elsewhere the Gold Coast was a doddle, very much a softer option. Even so with the diverse missives which were being sent from various parts of Whitehall, from the Free French Headquarters and even from America many 'cloak and dagger' organisations abounded not least of which was the one established by Ken and Jock. It was only by the insistence that nothing should be done to provoke French West Africa's neutrality that real trouble was prevented. Nevertheless, there were many local problems in Western Ashanti that had to be dealt with.

In between the problems time dragged in a routine sort of way. There were periods of inactivity and not much to keep the battalion (well some them) busy. Not Jock though.

He was very busy having established a black market enterprise and it wasn't too long before it was thriving. Oh yes, Jock seemed to be doing very nicely thank you. Ken had been persuaded to become the 'sleeping partner' so to speak, discreetly maintaining a record of goods and supplies. No one argued with Ken. There was an air about him, an officiousness, that would send a squaddie weak at the knees. He couldn't put up with disobedience, disrespect, nor discomfort although the latter was ameliorated by certain items from 'the stores' in return for the well-disciplined manner in which he ran 'the business'. Being a stickler for regulation and a well-ordered existence had probably influenced his promotion and as sergeant he was clearly adept at keeping the troops in line. When he barked an order, order there was and no mistake.

With the war going well, if indeed wars ever go well, the Allies had the upper hand with the exception of the heavy losses being sustained amongst the convoys in the Atlantic inflicted by torpedoes from scavenging U-boats. Elsewhere in Africa Tripoli was captured, Rommel had retreated in Tunisia pursued by the Allies although the 'Afrika Korps' had managed to mount a counterattack against the Americans at the Kasserine Pass. Patton had led his tanks into Tunisia and with the assistance of Montgomery the Germans retreated further to the north. In the Pacific all hell had broken loose and in Europe the Germans and the Russians (and a few other nations who had got involved) were massacring each other. Ken and Jock managed to successfully avoid all the action and took advantage of every opportunity anywhere they could.

By 1943 Jock McClean had decided that a couple of years was enough. The illicit enterprise was up and running and wanted out, and out of Africa in particular. His discharge didn't quite happen the way he might have wanted though.

Whilst on his way one night to keep a secret liaison with his latest female conquest he was accidentally thrown from his motorcycle whilst swerving to avoid running into a sergeant who had 'appeared out of nowhere'. That was his story anyway. Some said he'd thrown himself from the motorcycle. Some said it was far from coincidental that it should have been 'his' sergeant he was swerving to avoid. Some said the sergeant was complicit in this so-called accident. Jock's injuries were fairly superficial with nothing more than a few abrasions and a greenstick fracture of his radius, but given the smooth-talking bastard that he was he was able to persuade the Medical Officer that he was no longer of any use to the army and should be classified Category D – unfit for military service. Some said it was all a put-up job. Some said he'd never been any use to the army anyway and were glad to see the back of him. So Jock was on the next troop ship back to England. It was no coincidence that so was Ken, but he was on authorised leave. It had taken some doing to get furloughed and onto the same liberty ship as Jock, but all part of their greater strategy. Exercising the utmost discretion, the sergeant and the private had clandestine meetings at every opportunity contriving how they would establish their 'market' business back in the UK.

Albert and Mabel were surprised but delighted nevertheless when Ken turned up at home. He apologised for not letting his folks know he was coming but they accepted his excuse that communication was difficult, telephone was out of the question, there was no airmail, and any letters sent by sea would take weeks to arrive, if at all being at the mercy of the U-boats. Ken could not believe the hardships that his parents had had to endure. He was of course aware that rationing of bacon, butter and sugar had been introduced during 1940 even before he left school. He was unaware that by 1942 rationing had been extended to pretty much everything else, petrol, all foodstuffs and clothes. It was particularly irritating and frustrating that back in Ashanti, he and Jock had somehow contrived to amass plentiful supplies of everything which they then sold to all and sundry at an extortionate price and enormous profit. The more Ken thought about it, the more he was determined to get the business up and running back home.

By May of 1943 during Ken's leave, the 'Dambuster' raids had denied the German war industries in the Ruhr Valley the electrical power they required. The majority of U-boats had been withdrawn and, given the few 'available' men that there were, Ken had encountered no problem in persuading a local land-army girl, Helen Robinson, that he was her man! By day Helen worked on the local farm just outside the village owned by Frank Waring. By night, walks across the farmland and frolics in the hay barn became a regular feature. For the duration of his leave there wasn't a day went by when the two of them weren't in each other's company. The weekly visit to the cinema followed by the walk home was always a highlight. What's more Helen was demonstratively proving that she had a way with Ken that repressed the worst excesses of his explosive volleys of rage. She seemed to have the ability to wrap him around her little finger. Albert and Mabel were all in favour of the relationship not so much from the calming influence that Helen had but more particularly since they were now assured a regular supply of fresh eggs and vegetables.

Before re-joining his regiment Ken proposed marriage. It had been a whirlwind romance but Helen accepted without hesitation although she did wonder what her parents Joe and Liz would make of it. Yes they were young but with a war on the future was uncertain and marriage was not something to be delayed any longer than necessary. Mabel was delighted at the prospect of a daughter-in-law although

Albert didn't really express any opinion or emotion one way or another.

The day came for Ken to return to Africa and with the news that the 'Afrika Korps' had surrendered to the Allies who had taken over a quarter of a million prisoners, and with the bombing by the Allies of Sicily and Italy there was speculation with regard to a forthcoming invasion of Europe and Ken was keen to get back and take over Jock's private enterprise.

Helen borrowed Farmer Frank's Austin 7 and drove Ken to Leicester London Road where he was to catch the train to London and then on to Southampton. As the young lovers stood there on platform two, totally oblivious of the hustle and bustle around them, never had parting been such sweet sorrow. Ken promised to stay safe and Helen vowed to stay pure. They agreed that whatever Joe and Liz might have to say they would marry when Ken next returned on leave.

With Ken restored to the war effort, or his part in it at least, which involved amassing all manner of illicit goods, life in the rural undulating green and leafy Midlands' countryside continued in a way of life to which all those at home were becoming accustomed. The eventual outcome of war hung in the balance. Helen and her folks Joe and Liz would sit around the wireless after their meagre supper (albeit with fresh veg, more often than not) to listen to the news on the Home Service. Occasionally they'd do similarly round at Albert and Mabel's house. All too often the newsreader would give you reasons to be optimistic, and then dash them with doom and gloom in the very next report. Helen sometimes went to the pictures with some of the land-army girls and she was especially looking forward to seeing the new Humphrey Bogart movie *Casablanca*. She had a new pair of silk stockings that had been given to her by a very presumptuous and pushy Scotsman; the driver of the

Midland Red bus which had taken her into town a couple of weeks previous.

The pushy Scotsman was none other than Jock McClean who, in the interests of maintaining a front of respectability had lied about his age to get the driving job. He was also making regular trips to North Yorkshire in a dark green Morris 10cwt van he borrowed from Ron Nicholls, a Midland Red conductor with whom he was often partnered. No one knew why he went or where he got his petrol coupons from either.

Early January 1944 welcomed the news that General Eisenhower was in London and was to become the Commanding General US Forces European Theatre of Operations. Why 'theatre'? Helen wondered. Not the sort of theatre I'd want to visit she thought. Hey-ho! There was rarely any news of what if anything was going on in Africa since the business in Libya had been sorted. Specifically news from the Gold Coast was conspicuous by there being none. A letter from Ken was a very rare but nevertheless a welcome treat every once in a blue moon. "Here's looking at you kid," he had remarked in his last missive. At least it made Helen smile.

February came and working on the land was certainly a challenge. Keeping warm, even more so. Then came confirmation of the plan for the invasion of Europe, 'Operation Overlord'. Could this be the beginning of the end or merely the end of the beginning?

Helen would make a detailed study of the casualty reports in the *Daily Herald* as soon as Joe had finished with it. It was always a relief to see no mention of Ken or even of his regiment. No news was surely good news? Then with the announcement that a certain Charles de Gaulle whoever he might be was to take command of the Free French Forces, and of busy preparations for D-Day all over southern England there must have been a blue moon for a letter arrived.

All being well, Ken wrote, in a very neat hand it must be said, *I'll be coming home on leave sometime in May.* When in May? How could she mark off the days on the calendar if she didn't know when? Despite the slight exasperation of the not knowing Helen was beside herself with excitement. Just another month and she would see her Ken.

May came. Ken didn't. 'Heavy bombings of the Continent'. '"Overlord" scheduled for 5 June'. 'King George VI, Churchill, Eisenhower, Patton, Montgomery' and Uncle Tom Cobley no doubt 'meet in London for D-Day briefings'. June 5th '"Overlord" begins'. '5,000 tons of bombs dropped on German gun positions on Normandy Coast'. June 6th '155.000 Allied troops land on Normandy beaches'. And so, the headlines continued. Where oh where was Ken?

Any euphoria there may have been about Ken's imminent return or the D-Day landings was totally eclipsed when the *Herald* announced in June that it was Hitler's belief that he could still win the war with the deployment of his secret weapon the V-1 Flying Bomb. These so-called 'vengeance' weapons kept coming with devastating effect sometimes with horrifying losses of life. But fortunately for folk in the Midlands the limited range of the V-1 meant that they never got much further than London or the southeast.

More horrifying for Helen, was the death of her father. He'd been unwell almost from when war was declared. The coughing and spluttering, the shortness of breath were all getting progressively worse. Then, on 25th August, with the announcement that Paris had been liberated from German occupation, Joe coughed his last. It wasn't the war that did for him, it wasn't a bomb or a bullet, it was the Woodbines! The cause of death recorded on his death certificate was Chronic Obstructive Pulmonary Disease. He was buried after a short family service at St Catherine's Parish Church and buried in the churchyard. At the graveside were Helen, her mum Liz, her sister Rosemary and her brothers John, Charlie, Sid and Frank. At a discreet distance beneath the shade of a great yew tree were Albert and Mabel.

Another harvest, another Christmas and another new year. The Allies had just about got the Germans surrounded on all sides and Hitler was holed up in his bunker in Berlin but demanding that his troops continued to fight with no retreat. Mussolini had been shot and the Soviets had entered Auschwitz. The horrors being discovered in the so-called death camps were reaching the wider world. This was surely the beginning of the end.

Chapter Two

As the spring of 1945 sprung Helen was busy with the new-born lambs on the farm. One morning and taking her completely by surprise Albert came rushing into the shed dropped his bike to the ground startling the sheep and more animated than she'd ever seen him.

'You've got a telegram!'

'What?'

'You've got a bloody telegram! Here read it for goodness sake'.

Helen washed her hands in a bucket dried them on her overalls and with trembling fingers took the flimsy blue paper from Albert. She carefully tore it open and with tears then smiles she read out loud.

'Dearest : stop: Home in May: stop: for god: stop: all my love: stop: Ken.'

Albert took the telegram from her and re-read it to himself and his indignation was unmistakable.

'Cheeky young bugger! Home in May? We've bloody heard that one before! And what's this, '*for god*'? What's he mean for bloody god? I'll give him bloody god!" With which he handed the telegram back to Helen picked up his bike and left huffing and puffing.

Helen's initial elation had somewhat evaporated when

Farmer Frank came into the shed, belching smoke from his pipe like an LMS 'Jinty' class tank engine. He'd heard Albert's outburst and was concerned.

'What's all the rumpus, gal?' Frank never had lost his Black Country drawl.

Helen handed him the telegram. Frank fumbled his glasses out of his bib-and-brace overalls, one arm of his specs bound up with a piece of Elastoplast. He perched them on the end of his nose and studied the message.

'I reckon it's a error. I reckon 'e means fer good, not fer god.' He drew on his pipe and pondered. 'Aye, that's it for definite. He means fer good! Yer man's coming 'ome, gal!"

Frank chugged away on his pipe and beamed at his bemused labourer.

That evening as soon as she'd cleared up after tea with her mum she rushed round to see Albert and Mabel. They were listening to the wireless. *Much Binding in the Marsh* was just finishing. Albert reached across from his armchair and switched the wireless off.

'So what do you make of it?' Albert asked, meaning the telegram.

'Well, I think Frank might be right. Perhaps he did mean 'for good' and the telegraph operator must have misheard him or something. I hope so anyway. When he wrote last year to say he was coming home in May, well, maybe he meant this May.'

'Ah that is as *may*-be.' Albert like a play on words. 'We'll have to wait and see.'

'He'll just turn up out of the blue like last time' Mabel interjected. 'You'll see.'

Notwithstanding the 'will he won't he' turn up quandary, May 1945 was a time of great excitement, not just locally but throughout the country. It had been announced on the wireless that a senior German General had made a request to cross the British lines in order to negotiate a surrender of all German land forces. News had broken that Hitler had committed suicide having appointed Goebbels as Reich Chancellor. He too then committed suicide having murdered his children first. The war in Italy was over, all U-boats had been ordered to cease operations then on May 7th Germany unconditionally surrendered to the Allies in Rheims, France. May 8th was designated VE Day. Victory in Europe.

It was around this time that the discovery of the Kaiseroda Salt Mine, in Merkers-Kieselbach became public knowledge. All the deposits in the Nazi Reichsbank had been moved to the mine for safekeeping. But the mine contained much more. Wedding rings and gold fillings of Jewish prisoners and Holocaust victims had been melted down and recast as ingots or gold bars of which there were over 8000 boxes. Fifty-five boxes of silver bullion were also uncovered. Additionally there were all manner of paintings and artworks that had been looted by the Nazis during the course of the war. Much of the treasure 'disappeared'. Some to the Vatican Bank, some to Swiss National Bank and some to various other European banking institutions.

VE celebrations erupted not just in the village but throughout the western world. People were taking to the streets in their thousands. For days and nights there were street parties and dancing and 'all manner of goings-on' according to Mabel. Albert quoted from Churchill's speech as reported in the paper – "We may allow ourselves a brief period of rejoicing as Japan remains unsubdued." American President Truman had also added a note of caution – "It's a victory only half won."

'Well the Yanks'll soon do for the bloody Nips . They're not going to stop me going up the Keys and that's a fact.' And, as if to prove a point Albert grabbed his cap and stomped off to the Cross Keys.

For the next few hours Helen and Mabel sat chatting away wondering when Ken would be back and even if he would back. They had no idea that his homeward journey would be delayed by the need to make a detour through the Soviet held state in central Germany. Mabel took an old biscuit tin from the bureau and removing the lid proudly showed Helen her son's Eastfield Secondary Modern School leaving certificate and a few photographs of Ken as a lad. They discussed how when and where the wedding should take place and whether they could start making arrangements without actually consulting the groom-to-be. Little did Mabel know, Helen had already got everything planned down to the last detail.

Through the next few weeks more and more soldiers, sailors and airmen were returning home and whenever she could she would borrow Frank's Austin and drive to Leicester hoping to catch sight of any returning Highlanders in their distinctive 'Glengarry' bonnets. Any one of them might have news or information on Ken's movements.

'Ye can't keep using up me petrol coupons lass. I'm sure 'e'll be 'ome when 'e's good an' ready. Just be patient. Bide yer time.'

In her heart Helen knew that Frank was absolutely right. Ever since she'd known him, and it hadn't been very long, Ken had not been the most communicative of people. Mabel always said that as a boy he very rarely had much to say. Would he ever come home? Helen wondered.

Chapter Three

It was June 1st. Helen was in the farmyard clearing the last of the muck from the sheep pens. Frank was sat on a straw bale watching her every move and smoking his pipe. Suddenly,

'Eh up, what's this then?'

He stood up and, with the stem of his pipe gestured towards a lorry coming up the lane towards the farm. Helen turned and immediately registered that this was no ordinary lorry. This was a khaki coloured Bedford QLT and before Frank knew what was going on she was running towards it.

Ken was home! He jumped down from the truck almost before it had come to a halt. Helen ran into his open arms and held on to him as if her life depended on it. Frank was walking towards them grinning and applauding. The driver of the truck, a lance-corporal,

made a three-point-turn in the lane, honked the horn and drove off leaving a kit bag and quite a large parcel on the verge and his erstwhile passenger in an embrace reminiscent of a scene from *Gone With The Wind*.

They walked up the lane towards the farm his arm around her shoulders her arm around his waist. Frank's rolling gait was fifty yards ahead and he disappeared into the farmhouse. He reappeared with three glasses and a bottle of Everard's finest from the Southgate Street Brewery. After this brief reunion celebration Frank's Austin was commandeered and Ken drove off almost forgetting to pick up his kitbag and parcel. Hopefully his folks would be pleased to see him, the Prodigal Son, and especially when they saw the contents of the parcel. He was also anxious to get out of his uniform, into his demob suit and meet up with Helen later.

'Hello Mam, whatcha, dad!' Mabel all but had a touch of the vapours.

'Kenneth! I just knew you'd be back. I'll put the kettle on,' she gasped.

'How do son. Welcome home' said Albert, never one to be over-demonstrative.

They sat for a while drinking tea, the parents attempting to elicit responses from their son on all manner of information regarding what had or hadn't transpired over the last couple of years, but with very limited success.

'I've brought you a present, a few things I thought you could use.' Ken picked up the parcel and placed it on the kitchen table. Mabel excitedly ripped the brown paper and the carboard carton open. There was revealed a jar of jam, half-a-pound of lard, and of butter, a two-pound bag of sugar, a quarter of tea, a tin of corned beef, more than several rashers of bacon carefully wrapped in greaseproof paper. There were various other items too, all of which had been in short supply or rationed for such a long time.

'And this is for you dad.' Ken said handing him a bottle of whisky. 'Oh and there're these, I almost forgot.' Ken reached into his tunic pocket and with the flourish of a magician produced a book of clothing coupons. Mabel was dumbfounded.

'Where on earth did all this lot come from?' She was quite bewildered.

'Better you don't know, so don't ask.' Ken cautioned.

'If it's not honestly acquired we don't...' Ken immediately jumped in before his dad could finish his sentence.

'Come on Dad, all's fair in love and war.' He was on the defensive. 'If you don't want it, I'll soon find someone that does!' Ken's tone was a sure sign that he thought his parents were being unreasonably ungrateful. He went to his room leaving the ill-gotten gains where they were. He had a wash, lay on the bed and slept for a couple of hours. When he woke he dressed in a clean shirt, tie and his navy-blue demob suit. To his relief the fit wasn't too bad. He took his new Omega watch from his tunic and checking the time, strapped it to his wrist.

'Time now for Helen,' he said to himself.

It was a lovely balmy evening with barely a breath of wind and the scent of apple and cherry blossoms in the air. Ken and Helen sauntered hand in hand along the bridle ways and footbaths around the village. They spoke little, just happy to savour every moment they were together having been apart for so long. As the twilight faded they stopped at the Cross Keys and took their drinks into the garden. Albert was amongst the few in the public bar and gave them a wave. Helen wanted to ask about the war, North Africa and all that he had been through as a soldier. She wanted to know where the very expensive looking watch on his wrist had come from but Ken didn't want to talk about any it. Helen gave up with the questions. After a while of gazing at each other and a conversation of sweet nothings Ken escorted his love home.

It didn't take many days before thoughts were turned to the marriage. Albert, Mabel and Liz were all too familiar with what Helen wanted on her wedding day. All that was required was for the groom-to-be to agree to what she had planned. When Helen broached the general outline of her wedding day she was relieved by the lack of resistance. So with the details finalised, a week later Ken and Helen were married at St Catherine's Parish Church. Joe was sadly missed of course but Frank made a splendid job of giving Helen away. In fact almost everyone remarked upon how well he'd scrubbed up for the occasion. Rosemary was Helen's bridesmaid, and Ken's brother Keith was best man. The wedding guests were mainly family and close friends plus a few regulars from the Cross Keys. With the ceremony concluded the bride and groom posed by the lychgate for a photographer; Helen in a long white gown, and Ken in full dress uniform including the kilt of course. After all the respective hardships, the sacrifices, disasters, calamities and adversity that everyone had endured during the war, it was a completely joyous day. The celebrations went on long into the night.

Members of the family were remarking that the newly married couple would have nowhere to live. Helen admitted that it was about the only flaw in her plans, but unbeknown to anyone, Ken had it covered. For weeks now Jock had been storing the goods in what was to become the marital home. Every fortnight a dark green Morris 10cwt loaded to the limit of its springs would deliver to ground-floor rooms in a private house in a quiet cul-de-sac.

The subterfuge was beautifully camouflaged even further when Rosemary, who was already married to an airman not due to be demobbed until later in the month, offered the spare bedroom in her house. Yes it was small, just a two up and two down mid-terrace with 'facilities' in the back yard. But it would only be for a week or two until a more permanent arrangement could be made, she had suggested.

The day after the wedding, Helen and her new husband were driven to Leicester London Road by Frank, in the Austin which he'd decorated non-too-skilfully with white ribbons. The newlyweds were to catch the train to Derby. From there a local bus would take them to High Tor, a small hotel in the Peak District for a short honeymoon; short by necessity. Ken was to start a job he had secured with a light engineering firm as a toolmaker and Frank needed Helen back on the farm.

June passed into July. The war in Japan was still raging and despite Churchill, Stalin and Truman's collective insistence on Japan's unconditional surrender the conflict continued. In the leafy Midlands villages life was returning to the new normal. Normal however was to take on a new meaning for Helen. Frank had become aware of her needing to take an increasingly frequent breather from her labours on the farm and she was experiencing some queasy mornings as well. Frank was fairly sure that Helen was expecting. Frank knew a thing or two. He was a farmer after all! The pregnancy was confirmed and at Frank's insistence, Helen's days as a land-girl were numbered and she was on 'light duties' with immediate effect.

Helen was absolutely delighted with her condition. Ken was less than enthusiastic or so he seemed. He was annoyed with himself. He should have been more careful. Living at his sister-in-law's with three others was becoming stressful especially the morning queue in the backyard. Adding a baby to the mix would exacerbate the situation to beyond intolerable. It hadn't been long at all before Ken was getting quite irritable and snappish. Every night he'd ask if there had been any message left for him. Every night the answer was in the negative. Every night he disappeared to the Cross Keys just to get out of the way. There were matters pressing on Ken's mind. Yes, the honeymoon was over, and, quite apparently, was the 'honeymoon period'.

The local paper was published every Friday. Ken would come home from work and pore over and over the 'Announcements' column in the classified section. But the message he was waiting for wasn't printed, week after week.

Then one week there it was. *Don't forget the keys, Sarge!*

That was it. The notice he'd been anxiously waiting for. He was off on his bike even before his tea.

In a mood of confident anticipation, even excitement, Ken biked to the Cross Keys to meet with he who had posted the 'coded' announcement, Jock. Even before Ken had returned to the UK he'd briefed Jock on the need for 'premises'. That brief had been subsequently amended to 'premises and accommodation' after the marriage proposal. With pints in hand they were straight down to business. Ken needed to hear what Jock had found. Not only would Jock's news impact on Ken's married life, there was the 'business' to consider. Jock reported that he had rented the ground floor of a semidetached house in a quiet cul-de-sac. All requirements were covered, accommodation and storage. It all sounded too good to be true and that would prove to be the case sooner rather than later. Ken and Helen could move in right away. Helen would be delighted Ken thought. It was time to toast their future success, and large measures of scotch were ordered.

It was ages before he got back to Rosemary's. Helen was getting quite concerned.

'Where've you been, I've been worried.'

'Celebrating!'

'Celebrating what exactly? Somewhere to live I hope!' It was Rosemary, just back from the farm. She and her husband Neville were also growing tired of being cooped up with their 'guests' in the small terraced house.

'Exactly!' slurred Ken, and holding his hand aloft with an imaginary glass in a mock toast. 'Thank you Rosemary, thank you Neville for your hospitality. We're moving out.'

Whilst the news was good in one sense Helen had been rather hoping she could have had a look at the property before they committed to it.

Chapter Four

The following week, the beginning of August, they moved into their home in the cul-de-sac. The house was fine although there were lots of flies in the hallway and it smelt fetid. Helen put it down to the house having been unoccupied for a period. There was much more space than at Rosemary's. An indoor toilet. No more suffering the indignities of the thunder-box! There was bathroom too and a separate kitchen which looked out over a small garden with a plum tree. There was also a spare room and an outhouse but both of these were locked. Ken said he'd contact the landlord to see about getting some keys.

On the Friday of that week Ken came home from work and sat down to read the local paper as he had been doing for weeks. There it was again, in the Announcements column. *Don't forget the keys, Sarge!*

The prearranged cloak and dagger signal from Jock was to let Ken know there were further developments they should meet to discuss. Just as on the previous occasion Helen was about to serve up his tea when he rushed out.

They met right on opening time at the Cross Keys. Ken bought the beers and they retreated to a small alcove which would normally be occupied by courting couples where they could whisper sweet nothings without fear of there being any eavesdroppers; as indeed Ken and Helen had done just weeks earlier. Confidentiality was paramount. Ken and Jock regarded their business affairs as being in the same classified league of top-secret plans as those for Operation Overlord had been.

They greeted each other in the manner of old mates which of course they were. But even so their greeting was very much in the suspicious and surreptitious manner of co-conspirators in a Shakespearean tragedy. They reviewed the many various contacts they had made over recent years, servicemen and civilians alike all 'in the market for a quick profit'. The war had been good for the two Eastfield Secondary Modern lads. Jock reported the wealth of loot which he had 'rescued' during air-raids and how he'd been obtaining books of counterfeit rationing coupons. More pints of beer were ordered and the state of the current situation was considered further. The shipment of crates from abroad by untraceable circuitous routes overland, by sea and by air had been arriving regularly and generally without any hitches The riskier cargoes of guns, grenades and ordnance that had been liberated from German prisoners had been delivered by the British Army no less to a fictional quartermaster, a Captain K Blake QM, for collection at Catterick. These had been collected in a dark green Morris 10cwt van from the Bourlon Barracks every other week. American cigarettes, bourbon, nylons that Ken had been stealing from the Allies had been shipped and collected. The wine route, courtesy of the French Resistance was secure and flowing freely and so it went on. Finally Jock announced that all goods were safely lock away in the cul-de-sac house and he jingled a set of keys before Ken's eyes, the keys to the spare room and outhouse. The one shipment still outstanding was from the Thuringia district of Germany. But they were confident it would turn up. This called for more beer which was summarily ordered forthwith.

'So where do you reckon we should go from here?' Ken asked.

'Aye well, we've a wee problem t'deal wi' first.'

'And what might that be?'

'We got a couple o' stiffs te dispose of.'

'What do mean, 'a couple o' stiffs'?' Ken's voice was raised mocking Jock's dialect.

'Keep ye bloody voice doon man.' Jock explained, "There's two did bodies upstairs."

Ken was apoplectic, his exasperation smouldering.

'How the hell…?'

Jock was attempting to explain in a calm and calculated manner. Ken was fuming just below the point at which he would explode; a rabid dog foaming at the mouth.

'Sit doon sarge.' Jock issued the stage-whisper through clenched teeth.

Jock continued with his stage-whisper and it was beginning to attract attention from other drinkers.

'I hid nay choice sarge. I hid t' shoot 'em.'

Ken was now beside himself with rage. He grabbed Jock by the lapels of his Midland Red uniform jacket and dragged him out of the alcove knocking glasses and furniture over as he did so. The landlord bawled from behind the bar,

'Out, out, get out the pair of you before I call the police!'

The scuffle spilled through the front door and on to the pavement. It was hardly a fair contest. Jock at five feet two inches, and eleven stone, wet through, Ken over six feet and fourteen stone. Jock took a massive hit to his head and went down like a sack of shit. Ken stood back, breathing heavily, poised for his next move. Lying prostrate and disabled on the ground, Jock was gasping for breath, wiping his bloody lip and nose on his sleeve.

'Ahm so sorry Ken. I kin explain. Please let me explain.'

Ken couldn't begin to fathom what explanation there

could be but decided to hear it anyway. He pulled Jock up from the pavement and sat him on the bench outside the pub. He went back into the bar and, apologising profusely to the landlord he requested a glass of water which he was given, albeit reluctantly.

'Aren't you Albert's son?' asked the landlord.

'I am, and again I'm sorry. I've just had some bad news and I'm a bit stressed.' Ken, now a little more composed offered this understatement by way of an excuse for his behaviour.

'Ah well, don't take it out on your little mate. Pick on someone your own size. I thought you were going kill him!' the landlord joked and continued serving other customers. Ken went outside and sat next to Jock offering him the glass of water.

'Well,' he demanded. 'Let's hear it then.'

Jock explained how, unbeknownst to him the upstairs tenants had been observing the dark green Morris 10cwt making its frequent deliveries. They had kept a diary with a description of the various crates and boxes on each occasion. Then on the last time he'd made a drop, the couple who Jock had previously assumed were a married couple, but who were in fact two men, confronted him. Cutting the long story short, Jock wasn't prepared to concede to their blackmail attempts and offer them the percentage they were demanding. Neither was he prepared to pay a one-off sum for their silence. When they threatened to inform the police, Jock gave the impression that he had given in, and went inside to their upstairs rooms to thrash out a deal he had no intention of agreeing and shot them both dead.

'Nothing but bloody crooks, so they wis!'

So there they were. Jock, a double murderer with a fat lip and a bloody nose and Ken, a recently married father-to-be, an accessory to murder. Were their dreams of a lucrative black market business all but shattered?

'What's to do then?'

'Let's gi 'n' hev another pint whilst we think on.' And they did – several.

Eventually Ken got home and despite his stupor and being barely able to think rationally he managed to let himself in. Helen had already gone to bed and he saw no point in waking her. So he lay on the sofa and in the knowledge of the heinous crimes that had been committed, crimes to which he was an accomplice, coupled with the drink-induced delirium tremens causing the room to spin, he lapsed into a psychotropic and hallucinatory nightmare featuring the two dead bodies that lay upstairs.

The following day, with a hangover from hell, he left for work but never arrived. He spent the whole day sitting on the bank of the canal, worrying, cursing, suicidal, all of which feelings were darkening his mood which was already violently savage.

The spare room was inexplicably kept locked. Helen was curious naturally enough but saw no reason to ask questions which she felt would only exacerbate Ken's increasingly snappy and waspish mood. Everything had been reasonably OK for a time although Ken's 'black dog' was never far away. Still she was mostly happy as the house was only a short walk from Frank's farm and she could pop round for a visit during the day whilst Ken was at work. But, the evenings, oh dear no. This is not what Helen had signed up for. She knew he was taciturn by nature but to sit in silence was taking it to extremes. He wouldn't even have the radio on. So they just sat until Helen went to bed usually on the verge of tears. Something was wrong. What had happened? Was it his new job? Was it the prospect of a baby? Was this to be the reality of married life? Surely not? Was it the content of the spare room?

The situation was rapidly deteriorating. Helen was now convinced that whatever the reasons for Ken's derangement and wretched despair, the cause lay behind the locked door of the spare room. Every time she raised the matter it provoked Ken into a burning rage. He often raised his hand to her and bouts of physical abuse had begun. Helen just couldn't understand why. Since they'd moved into the house she'd heard comings and goings at all hours of the night as she lay awake in bed. She suspected that Ken was involved in something nefarious and it was getting to the stage when she was fully expecting a knock on the door from the police. She was also getting completely fed up with being treated as nothing more or less than Ken's skivvy, cooking, cleaning, washing and ironing, more often than not without a single word of thanks. In her condition this was not acceptable. Liz, her mum had expressed her grave concern. She went to see Mabel but she merely attempted to make some pretty feeble excuses for her son's behaviour and attitude. What Mabel wouldn't admit to was that she was beside herself with worries having heard the Cross Keys gossip.

Chapter Five

'America Drops Atom Bomb on Japan'; 'Rain of Ruin'; 'Hiroshima Wiped Out' screamed the headlines on the news-stand. Helen had taken the bus into town but barely noticed the billboards. Whatever the Japanese survivors were suffering was of little consequence in Helen's world and her suffering. She was on her way to the pharmacy for some 'arnica'. The bruising on her face and arms would heal but she was self-conscious of any disfigurement however temporary. Besides which she didn't want to be making excuses to people who were bound to enquire how she had acquired such injuries.

As she passed the front of café at the bus station where the drivers and conductors took their tea breaks, the door was open and she heard a Scots brogue which she thought she recognised. She turned and looking at the short fellow leaning on the counter and holding forth on the situation in Japan, she wasn't sure but... wasn't that... she wondered. Upon noticing her looking in his direction the café's local political commentator piped down and walked towards her.

'Hello again,' he said. 'Are ye wanting the next bus? It's nae due for a few minutes yet.'

Before Helen could respond he continued.

'Did the stockings fit?' Instant recall! This was the bus

driver who had attempted to chat her up and gave her a pair of silk stockings.

'Isn't it Helen? Are ye nae Ken's new wife?'

'You know Ken?'

'Och aye. We were buddies here n there during the war. Well, more than buddies, more like partners really."

'Partners?' Helen queried.

'Aye we hid a little business between us.'

'What sort of business?' Helen was intrigued.

'Och just a wee bit o buying n selling. Tell Ken Jock says 'nae hard feelings'."

'I will," she said, curious. 'Nice to see you again.'

'Aye you too.

Helen turned on her heel and walked off on her mission to the chemist. A little later after completing a couple of other errands she was back at the bus stop.

'Well I never. Would ye fancy that? Seeing ye so soon.' Jock again. 'That's a nasty bruise ye have there,' he noticed. Helen's hand went to her face and she felt herself blushing.

'I hope Ken's nae knocking ye aboot,' he joked.

'Oh it's nothing, an accident,' Helen replied, wishing it had been.

'Aye I hid a similar 'accident' mysel' recently!" Jock said remembering the beating he'd received from Ken.

When Ken turned up at cul-de-sac house that evening, his mood was as black as ever. He washed his hands at the sink and slumped down at the kitchen table.

'What's for tea?' he demanded.

'I managed to get some lamb chops. I thought you'd like that.' Ken grunted his approval, or was it disapproval? It was impossible to tell which.

'Oh, and I met an old army friend of yours in town'. Helen was trying her hardest to be conversational but Ken was immediately on the defensive.

'Who?' Another aggressive demand.

'A small bloke. A Scotsman. He said to tell you 'Jock says no hard feelings'.'

An astute observer would have noticed Ken's hackles rise.

'Did he say anything else?'

'He said you were mates, no, partners. You had a buying and selling business.'

'The bloody haggis bashing bastard!' Ken cursed. Nothing further was spoken as the chops were served.

After tea and with more than a little trepidation Helen broached the 'partner's' description that Jock had used.

'None of your bloody business!' Ken's demeanour was threatening. Helen needed to know so she persisted.

'Is that where your watch came from? Were the two of you dealing on the black market? Is that what your folks' food parcel was? Black market? Was it? Tell me! What's in the spare room?' Helen's line of questioning was becoming much more urgent and demanding. Ken raised his fist and unleashed a body blow which winded Helen.

'I told you, none of your bloody business!' Ken went out into the garden slamming the door behind him.

Helen was hurting but in her anger she fought back the tears whilst panting hard to regain her breath. She took a long hard look at herself in the mirror which hung over the fireplace and determined there and then that she wasn't going to put up with any more of the domestic abuse she was suffering. If need be she was quite prepared to inform the police and not just about violence either. But first she'd try and talk to Jock a little more. Maybe he'd be a bit more forthcoming about the nature of their 'business'. Maybe he could shed some light on the monster that Ken had become.

It was a Wednesday evening. The meal had been a disaster. The chops clearly hadn't been to Ken's liking since he threw his plate to the floor, describing it as unfit for a dog.

Helen had burst into tears and Ken disappeared into the bedroom. He emerged a half-an-hour later dressed in a suit that Helen had not seen before. Ominously, he was carrying a hold-all.

'I'm going away,' he announced. 'I can't stay here.'

'Where to? How long for? What do you mean, you can't stay here?'

'It's better you don't know.'

'Will you be back for the baby?'

'Maybe, maybe not,' was the answer. Much to Helen's surprise, he gave her a peck on her cheek, which somehow had a finality about it. He left the house slamming the door behind him. Not that she realised it at the time, but that was the penultimate time Helen would see Ken.

Chapter Six

With the slamming of the front door Helen's cogitative faculties ran through the whole gamut of emotions. She didn't know what to think, she didn't know what to do. So she poured herself a glass of whisky and sat at the kitchen table almost in a state of suspended animation. She didn't drink whisky. She didn't even like whisky. She went to bed.

The next morning, early, feeling that she didn't have a friend in the world that she could turn to, she decided to take a walk. The sun was shining but the leaves were turning and autumn was in the air. Helen hadn't consciously thought about where she was headed and unconsciously followed her well-trodden path to the farm. Frank was in the yard, scratching his head and swearing at the old Massey Harris 744. He greeted Helen with a smile and open arms. She ran into his arms and burst into tears.

'Ee, c'mon lass, whatever's up?' Helen's wailing continued unabated. She made no response.

'Nowt can be that bad can it?' This time she responded.

'Oh Frank' she sobbed, 'whatever am I to do?'

'Well you can start by drying your eyes an' telling me all about whatever's wrong over a cup-a-tea.'

They went into the kitchen. As always the kettle was simmering on the Aga and the teapot was soon on the table.

Helen recounted chapter and verse of her married life with a detailed account of the recent happenings leading up to Ken's departure. During her narrative Frank had lit his pipe whilst listening hard to what he was being told. He stared into her face and could now see that some of the redness around her eyes was not entirely

as a result of the tears.

'As old as I am I'll 'ave 'im! I'll not have any man lay a finger…" He huffed and puffed. Since Joe had died, Frank had been Helen's surrogate father. He was very fond of her.

'No Frank, violence won't do. It won't get us anywhere. Besides, the way I feel at the moment if I never see him again it'll be too soon. There's no way I'll have him back.'

After a few moments of an awkward silence Helen started to cry again.

'I can't stay here in the village. What will people think? I can't pay the rent anyway. I've no money and he's not left me any.' Frank puffed on his pipe.

'You're right of course. I dint mean I'd 'it 'im. It were just, how's it called, a figure of speech? Don't you be worryin' about money. I tek yer point about not stayin' in village though. But it ain't just you now, is it? We've got the little un to think about in a few months time. What's going to happen to that poor little beggar?' That was a question weighing all too heavily on Helen 's mind and to which there were no answers readily forthcoming.

'Let me see if I can't sort summut out.'

Helen followed Frank out into the yard and left him to his attempts to get the tractor started. She decided a walk might clear her head and went to see Mabel although she wasn't entirely sure whether talking to Ken's mother at this time was such a good idea.

Later that evening as she sat with a corned beef sandwich, the wireless was on but she wasn't really listening to it. She was worrying about whatever it was in the spare room. Then there was a knock at the door. Helen hesitated. Had Ken come back? Was he going to apologise? Would everything be OK again? Another knock at the door, more insistent this time. If it was Ken did she really not want to see him? If it wasn't Ken who could it be? Was it the police? She went to door and called out.

'Who is it?'

'It's me lass, Frank. C'mon open the door.' Relief! Frank came in and gave Helen a box of Cadbury's Milk Chocolates he'd been hoarding since before the war.

'Thought these might cheer you up a bit. Now I've had a word with me little brother. He's got nearly 400 acres near Kilby Bridge. He's also got an empty cottage on 'is farm you can 'ave, rent free for as long as. 'is daughter Kate, my niece, she'll be able to look after you when yer time comes."

'Oh Frank I don't know what to say. What's his name, your brother?'

'Ernest. It were us dad's joke – Frank and earnest.' He laughed. "Good job we 'aint got a Sidney in the family else we'd 'ave Kate and Sidney as well." She had to think about Frank's joke for a moment but then Helen was laughing too.

'It's agreed then?'

'Agreed!'

And so it was. When she was ready to leave Frank would take Helen and all her belongings to Kilby Bridge. Her new location. Her safe house would be their secret.

Helen thought that she really should let her mother know her intentions. She didn't want her worrying but she didn't relish the idea of swearing her mother to secrecy. The fewer the number of people who knew her whereabouts the less the likelihood of Ken finding out.

Helen spent the next few days sorting stuff out. She didn't know who the landlord was but she left him written notice optimistically enclosing a £5 note she'd borrowed from Mabel in the hope that it would be sufficient to cover whatever sum might be owed. Most of her own things, clothes and personal effects fitted into the one suitcase that they had used on the honeymoon trip; a trip she'd now like to forget. All of the clothes and things that Ken had left behind easily fitted into his army kitbag. She would ask Frank to deliver it to Albert and Mabel's house. With the house cleared all that remained to be moved was whatever was in the outhouse and the spare room; possibly the root of all the problems. She still didn't know what was in either place. The first problem would be gaining access. She'd ask Frank for his help.

The next day Frank came round in the car.

'Now then, let the dog see the rabbit; let's be 'avin' a look at what's what.' He examined the task.

'Good job I thought to put some tools in the car,' he said, and off he went to fetch them. With a minimum of exertion Frank had the hasp and clasp with the padlock still secured removed from the door and frame of the outhouse with hardly any damage for which Helen was grateful. They gingerly took a look. Then open-mouthed with incredulity at what they had seen, they went inside to the spare room. Frank worked his magic with his lock-picks and with far less caution than with the outhouse, heaved the door open having a much greater notion of what to expect.

'Bugger me!' he cried out. 'Sorry about me language,' he apologised. Helen took a look inside.

'Bugger me as well!' she gasped. It wasn't a big room, more a box room really, about ten feet square. But it was packed wall to wall and floor to ceiling. There were boxes and boxes of wine and spirits; 'Bells', 'Haig', 'Johnnie Walker', 'Gordons' and brands that even Frank had never heard of. Boxes of cosmetics and nylon stockings. Franked pulled a carton from the top of a stack and opened it. Cigarettes. 'Lucky Strike', 'Craven A', 'Players Navy Cut', 'Marlboro'. Boxes of foreign brands as well as the more familiar ones. There were cameras, top-of-the-range 35mm 'Zeiss', 'Canon', 'Leica'. There were watches, 'Omega', 'Rolex', 'Longines'. There were all manner of boxes and crates of wartime issue hardware, much of it German some of it Soviet. A wooden crate labelled 'Grossfuss Sturmgewehr' contained evil-looking assault rifles wrapped in oiled paper. Some crates looked as though they had never been opened. Then, on top of those there were other wooden boxes of handguns, 'Luger', 'Mauser', 'Walther', all brand new, packed in straw with large tin boxes full of ammunition.

'Bugger me!' Frank reaffirmed. Pointing at the weaponry he came out with "Das ist verboten, ja?" Almost comical in his Brummie dialect but Helen wasn't laughing. She was much more worried than impressed or amused

'I've never seen owt like this in me life! It's the bloody black market an' no mistake!' He was spluttering and of the hundreds of questions he clearly wanted to ask, he didn't know where to start. So he sat down on a case of 'Moet et Chandon'.

'An' there's all that outside an' all!'

The black market had been a response to the rationing that was introduced during the war. It was illegal. Nevertheless, it was a driving force. The Atlantic convoys had to run the gauntlet of the German U-boats resulting not only in thousands of tons of shipping being lost, but thousands of tons of imported goods and provisions ending up on the bottom of the ocean as well. The government was anxious that everyone on the Home Front should get a fair share of what was available. But if you could afford the prices, pretty much everything was available from the racketeers, the SPIVS – 'suspected persons and itinerant vagrants'. There was a great deal of money to made on the black market. Even the farmers were in on the act, being able to earn much more by selling on the black market, or to SPIVs than by selling to the government. Even Frank had a queue of folks at the barn door most days, hoping to buy vegetables and eggs. Helen had read somewhere that by 1945 there had been over 100,000 prosecutions. The penalties were severe but not sufficiently so to provide the disincentive for those who were making enormous profits. Even now with the conflict over servicemen were returning with the spoils of war and whilst they weren't necessarily black marketeers they were selling to the highest bidder. But for the hardened professional SPIV, looting, theft, and other means of an illicit acquisition of almost anything with a resaleable value had become a way of life. With the opening of this 'Aladdin's Cave' Helen had little doubt that her earlier suspicions that Ken was involved were confirmed.

Ken was not just a black marketeer Helen realised. That new suit, the watch, no, he was a SPIV of the worst kind. Profiteering from the hardships of others. Neither was he merely in the butter, jam and bacon league either. Judging by his stock he was a mogul, a captain of industry of the most illegal kind. She cast her mind back three or four weeks to the time she confronted him with what Jock had said about he and Ken being partners. What was it he'd said? Ah yes, 'none of your bloody business'. And thank goodness it isn't, she thought. Frank had been having a rummage.

'Well I don't know Helen. What're we going to do wi' this lot? We can't just leave it 'ere now can we?'

'I suppose not,' she conceded.

Helen then decided that there was no alternative than to take Frank, the only person she really trusted, into her confidence. Goodness knows she needed an ally and who better than Frank? She told him as much as she knew about Jock;

the partnership; about how she thought he fancied her, the silk stockings. It was obvious where they'd come from now. The two of them sat there staring into the store of illicit ill-gotten gains; the contents of this warehouse of felonious contraband; Frank perched on his champagne, and Helen on a case of scotch as they tried to make some sense of whatever it was that had led Ken to such devious crookedness and villainous racketeering.

After a great deal of thought Frank came up with a scheme.

'I'll come round tonight wi' tractor and trailer. We'll load all this 'ere hot stuff on the trailer, cover it wi' a sheet an' some sacking an' I'll hide it the barn until we know what to do.'

'Shouldn't we just inform the police and let them deal with it?' Now that suggestion plucked at the strings of Frank's conscience.

'I s'pose we should but I'd be willing to bet that they'd just divvy up the booze and fags between themselves and turn the guns and stuff over to the army. Let's just get it out of here first. It'll mean a lot of trouble fer you if it's all discovered in your house.'

It was the word 'trouble' that was sufficient to persuade Helen to go along with Frank's plan. And that's what happened. The entire crooked cargo was loaded onto the trailer unnoticed under the cover of darkness. It took them the best part of the night. The trailer was shunted into the barn at the farm where it was hidden behind heaps of straw bales. Helen turned a blind eye to the bottle of Macallan that made it into Frank's kitchen.

Chapter Seven

The bodies in the bedroom had been on Jock's mind and although he'd returned the Luger to the crate in the spare room the corpses and the murder weapon really needed to be disposed of. He accepted that it would be something he would have to do without assistance as well. Incriminating anyone else would only complicate the situation and increase the risk of him being found out not only as a murderer but as a partner in a multi-thousand pound black market racket.

He sat in the Cross Keys pondering his options, not that he had any.

'Get rid o' th' stiffs' he repeated to himself over and over. Then came the brainwave such as it was. Ken was gone goodness knows where and the wife he'd left behind was a potential problem as well. Anyway folks in the cul-de-sac were used to seeing a dark green Morris 10cwt van making night-time deliveries so a collection shouldn't arouse any suspicion either should it? Once the bodies had been 'buried' he could then concentrate on the 'stores' which after all represented his future and his fortune.

He borrowed Ron's van again in return for five pound's worth of counterfeit petrol coupons not that Ron knew they were fake. Fortified by a good long draught from a scotch bottle he climbed the stairs of the cul-de-sac house knowing that the bodies would be exactly where he'd left them. He decided to deal with the smaller of the two first. Being of a fairly diminutive stature himself Jock had great difficulty rolling the body to the top of the stairs. From there gravity came to his assistance. With the body at the bottom of the stairs, Jock went to the van to fetch the sack-barrow he'd had the presence of mind to steal from the railway station. Eventually after a monumental struggle and another swig of Scotch he'd loaded stiff number one into the van.

He sat on the bottom step and smoked a Woodbine before galvanising himself into dealing with stiff number two. The difficulty with stiff number two was equal to stiff number one plus three stone. It took a Herculean trial of strength to complete the task. He locked the house and sat behind the wheel of the van. Another Woodbine and more Scotch later he released the handbrake and coasted down the slope of the cul-de-sac only starting the engine when he was well clear.

Having been in the army Jock knew a thing or two about the importance of having a strategy. Had he indeed not been an unsurpassed master of collection and distribution? Earlier reconnaissance had determined how and where he would dispose of his unwanted passengers. He drove towards Leicester and onto the Upperton Road bridge which crossed the railway goods yard. During the day he had observed the unhitched empty goods wagons that extended all the way from the yard and under the bridge. It was four-o'clock in the morning. The street was deserted and it was a fairly straightforward job to disembark his 'passengers' from the van and over the bridge parapet into an empty goods wagon. The wagons would eventually be filled with coal or aggregate and be towed off to who-knows-where for good-ness-knows-what. So that was that, job done! With a clear conscience and an absence of even the merest tinge of guilt

Jock drove straight to the Midland Red depot to start his shift in the knowledge that his future was now assured and that he had got away with murder, probably.

Chapter Eight

Helen decided that Frank was putting himself at risk. By her assessment Helen considered the risk to be unacceptable and unreasonable. The last thing she wanted would be for Frank to be charged for receiving stolen goods or as an accessory to whatever the crimes were that Ken had committed. She had to do something but what exactly? If Ken and Jock had been partners shouldn't Jock now be taking responsibility for the 'business'? Helen made up her mind there and then that in the first instance she would find Jock and see what he had to say. What she did subsequently would be dependent on what he said.

The following day Helen caught the bus into town and alighted at the terminus. As usual, there were drivers and conductors in the café. She went in.

'Excuse me' Helen approached a conductress sitting at the table nearest the door.

'I'm looking for one of your colleagues. I think he's a driver, a Scotsman, about five-foot six...'

'Oh, you mean Jock?' The conductress responded before Helen could finish her description.

'Not got you in the family way has he?' She gestured towards Helen's slight 'bump' which was beginning to show. Helen blushed.

'No, nothing like that,' she responded.

'Anybody know what Jock's on?' the conductress shouted above the general hubbub.

'He's on the eleven ten from Leicester, should be here in a couple of minutes,' came the response.

'There you are' announced the clippie. 'Watch yourself with that one!'she advised with a wink.

'Oh I will, don't you worry and thanks for your help.' Helen went outside to wait for the eleven ten from Leicester.

When the bus pulled up several passengers got off then the conductor followed by the driver who was indeed, Jock.

'Well, hello again! I hope it's me yous waiting for.'

'I certainly am!' Jock's conductor was disappearing into the café.

'Get me one in Ron, I'll just be a wee while.' Jock shouted after him.

'There are several matters you and I need to discuss,' said Helen in a most business-like manner that rather took Jock aback.

'Could you meet me in the Cross Keys at seven this evening please?' she asked.

'Aye, I wull that. In fact I'll be glad to. It's the first time I've been asked oot by a real lady.'

'It's not a date,' she reprimanded, 'it's a very serious situation we have to resolve.'

Helen gave him a forbidding glower and left Jock standing open-mouthed.

'Yer tea's getting cold,' yelled Ron.

On the way home she contemplated upon what she might say, how her meeting with her husband's erstwhile partner ought to be handled. Whatever, whether an agreement was reached or not there had to be an action plan formulated for implementation forthwith. This was to be Helen's last night in the village before she 'disappeared' to Kilby Bridge.

Meanwhile and with the stub of a pencil about two inches long Frank had been doing some calculations. Before the war a bottle of scotch whisky cost around £1/0s/0d from the off-licence. At that price, he estimated he had about £14,000 worth of spirits in his barn. Just selling the spirits would keep him going for the best part of three years at least. As for the rest of the stuff he'd got no idea of its value or what it would cost legally. 'Guns, watches, cameras, goodness knows what anyone might be prepared to pay' he thought. Even so as far as his reckoning and limited thought processes had taken him Frank had worked out that an ordinary bloke with an average weekly wage of about £25 could live quite comfortably off the proceeds without lifting a finger for a long time – even longer!

It was about ten minutes to seven. Helen sat in the small lounge bar with a glass of tonic water. On a weekday evening this early there wouldn't be too many people about and whatever she had to say to Jock was unlikely to be overheard. He arrived just as the clock in St Catherine's church steeple began to chime. He ordered a glass of whisky and a half pint of bitter 'chaser' and came and sat opposite Helen.

'I'm intrigued, ye've really got me thinking lassie,' he began.

'Really?' questioned Helen. 'I'd have thought you would know full well what I need to talk to you about.' She attempted to educe a reaction from him.

'Ken has left me. I've no idea when he'll be back if at all and whether I would have him back if he did return from wherever it is he's gone to.' Nothing! No reaction at all. She continued.

'I'm leaving the village. I'm moving out tomorrow.' Again nothing!

'I've cleared the house.' Nothing! Helen couldn't believe it. She looked him straight in the eyes. Not a flicker. He was either a very good poker player or he genuinely had no idea of what had been in the spare room.

'Aye, well, the last time I saw Ken I knew there was something nae right wi' 'im. Ahm sorry te hear he's gone and left ye in the lurch but nae sure why ye'd want te involve me.'

'But I thought you were partners in some 'business' interest, or so you told me a few weeks ago.' Helen's emphasis on the word 'business' was loaded with implication.

'Aye, well we did de a wee bit o' dealing in, y'know, commodities that were hard te come by during the war.'

'So if you're honestly telling me that you have no idea of what was in my spare room I'll just let the police know and…' The reaction she'd been waiting for came like a lightning bolt.

'Now then just ye hold on there!' Jock interrupted, panic in his voice.

'I knew it!' Helen exclaimed, almost elated.

'I didnae say I knew. I just dinnae want the police sniffing aroond. They've a'ready been asking questions.'

'What sort of questions?' Helen was now curious.

'Well,' Jock leaned across the table and whispered in conspiratorial tones, 'apparently, a consignment of valuable 'items' has gone missing and they think some o' them might be in this area.' He thought it prudent not to say anything about missing persons.

'But you know nothing about them!'

'I didnae say that,' he repeated

'Look Jock I just want you to be honest with me.'

'Aye well it's perhaps better that ye know nothing. I cannae tell ye.'

'I know where these 'items' as you call them are, which is more than you do. If you're not prepared to tell me the truth I will call the police,' she emphasised.

'Aye, OK. Ye have me there,' Jock admitted. 'Ye win lassie' he conceded.

The conversation went on in similar vein for quite some time. Jock was talking in riddles and giving nothing away and by the time St Catherine's struck nine and Jock was on his fifth whisky and chaser all that they'd agreed was that Helen would assume whatever Ken's role had been. After all, she had no money, no income, no prospects and a baby on the way. She knew it was illegal but what other choice did she have? It was a calculated risk but she was smart and provided she was careful and able to keep Jock on a tight rein here was an opportunity to secure her future in the short term. Finders keepers, she told herself.

'I'm sure it's easier than it seems – or is it?' she thought. 'Only one way to find out.'

Ever the gentleman, Jock walked her back to the house which had been her home for such a short time. What had gone wrong? She still couldn't fathom what it was that had caused such a drastic change in Ken. Was he running away? Maybe the police were onto him for something or other. Could he be as big a crook as Jock? Surely not! What else could it

Chapter Nine

The following day was Jock's 'rest day' not that he spent it resting, far from it. He needed to arrange the removal of the 'stores' to somewhere safe, not that Helen had told him where the stores were but an isolated lock up of some description was needed as a matter of urgency. Jock reasoned that it could only be a matter of time before the local constabulary closed in. He had another plan. Firstly he needed a means of getting about. His various contacts in the nether regions of the underworld were spread fairly far and wide.

He cycled down to the bus depot where he hoped he would be able to beg, steal or borrow his conductor Ron's motorbike. The Land Army had been selling off the Ariel 350s they used throughout the war and Ron had recently bought one which he kept at the Midland Red depot. Ron, in common with most ordinary folk just after the war were susceptible to bribery even a little corruption. And so it was that the promise of a bottle of scotch and a carton of Woodbines was sufficient for Ron to furnish Jock with the use of a mode of transport.

Jock was no stranger to riding a motorbike. He'd ridden miles during the war. Off he went touring around the country lanes in an ever-increasing radius looking for deserted barns or farm buildings which might suit his purpose but without much success. Frustrated by his lack of progress and a morning wasted he decided to head back to the bus depot. He took the A5 Watling Street from Broughton and deciding to seek inspiration from a glass of beer stopped at the Lime Kilns, a pub right by the side of the road, nestling under a humped-back bridge over the Hinckley arm of the Ashby canal. He went into the pub and ordered a pint.

After a couple of sips, his attention was drawn to a narrowboat making its way up the cut from the wharf at Hinckley. He rushed outside and walked along the towpath keeping pace with the boat whilst staring at it. Whether it was something in the beer or merely coincidental, it was indeed the inspirational moment that had so far been missing.

'A bloody barge. That's the answer!' he spoke out loud. He ran back to the pub finished his beer and enquired of the landlord where he might acquire a narrowboat. The landlord replaced the glass he was polishing on the shelf and nodded in the direction of a chap sitting at the end of the bar nursing a pint pot and smoking a pipe.

'Arthur,' he called, 'chap here would like a word.' Jock soon discovered that Arthur had been the owner and skipper of a working boat during the war and only too happy to regale him with all the information he would need, and more. The next hour just disappeared as Arthur proudly relived his life as a boatman for Jock's edification. Canals had been used for carrying all manner of goods and supplies up and down the country during the war he explained. With the war over, road and rail transport were becoming increasingly popular and long-distance commercial traffic on the canals was diminishing. The more Jock heard the better he liked the plan which was hatching even as he listened to Arthur's tales. Jock was working it all out in his head. In general, canals were not very accessible as they wended their way through miles and miles of isolated countryside. There were bridges and tunnels and locks and all manner of places where a barge could hole up. A barge could hold any amount of cargo which could be quite easily disguised. The icing on this particular cake of a plan was that it wouldn't be too difficult to 'acquire' fuel. Buses ran on diesel and he knew where there was a source! Then there was the cherry on the top. Self-contained accommodation, and for two. His thoughts turned to his new 'business' partner. They could live on the boat, keep an eye on the 'stock' and by navigating up and down the canal network, keeping on the move, ducking and diving and run a profitable business buying and selling. Brilliant! He couldn't think of a single flaw in the plan. There was just one thing missing – and fairly crucial at that. He didn't have a boat. Still for a man of Jock's enterprise this difficulty could soon be overcome.

'So, Arthur let me get you another pint.' Another pint was ordered whether he wanted it or not. 'Where's your barge now? Would you consider selling it?'

'It's not a barge it's a narrowboat,' Arthur corrected Jock in a lugubrious sort of way. 'Was it the beer or was he just being anal?' Jock wondered.

'Barge, narrowboat, all the same to me,' said Jock.

'You won't get far as a boatman if you don't know the difference' advised Arthur.

Jock then had to listen to how the vessels differed and many of the finer points of life on 'the cut' as Arthur called the canal. Jock was sure he could persuade Arthur to part with his boat.

'Where's it parked? Would you like to sell it? Here, look let me get one in for you for this evening.'

'You don't park a narrowboat. You moor it.' More advice from Arthur.

'OK. Whatever, where's it moored?'

'Just down the arm here at the pub, the Wharf. You know it?' After another couple of pints, Jock was the proud owner of the *Emily Rose* a diesel-engined narrowboat for which he'd paid the very modest price of £100 in cash. Apart from the troop ships, he'd never been on a boat, never mind owned or skippered one.

'I can drive a bus. So how hard can it be on a boat?' he thought aloud. He would find out.

He left Arthur slumped at the bar. He kicked the Ariel into life and roared off to see Helen almost beside himself with excitement. He rode directly, if a little erratically under the influence of the several pints the negotiations had taken to the house to which he had escorted Helen the previous evening completely forgetting that she was moving. The problem was he didn't know where she was moving to. So, how was he to make contact with her as his 'partner'.

Chapter Ten

Helen was at the farm with Frank about to leave for Kilby Bridge. On the back seat of the Austin 7 were Helen's clothes and a few personal possessions and kitchen utensils. The sound of a motorbike gave the two of them cause to cast furtive glances firstly at each other and then back towards the barn. The motorbike appeared in the lane and drove straight into the farmyard. Jock switched off the engine, dismounted and pulled the machine up onto its stand.

'Thank goodness I found you. Your upstairs neighbour suggested ye might be here,' he lied with relief in his voice realising Helen would be unaware her neighbours' demise. 'And who might this old Sassenach be?' he enquired, extending his hand towards Frank.

'This is Frank and this here is Frank's farm.' Helen waved her arm in a wide arc encompassing the buildings and the land as far as the eye could see. She made the introductions in a semi-formal manner.

'Frank, this is Jock. Jock, Frank.'

'Aye, grand to meet you Frank. Any pal o' Helen's is a pal o' mine.' Jock was still holding out his hand. Frank was eyeing Jock with suspicion as he recalled what Helen had previously mentioned about him. Eventually Frank took

Jock's hand. The handshake was a firm one, not at all what Frank had been expecting.

'Grand, is it? I knows who you are an' I knows what you are. If ye so much as dare t'take advantage of my Helen…' The threat was real enough even though he didn't finish the sentence. Helen was flattered by Frank's use of the possessive pronoun.

'Dinnae worry yoursel' Frank. I've nae intention ay anything ay the sort." Frank was far from convinced but he could see from Helen's body language that she had some kind of arrangement with this 'bloody porridge gunner', as Frank thought of him Anyway, he had no intention of upsetting the cart, either metaphorically or in reality.

" 'I s'pose we could all use a cuppa.' Frank led the way into the kitchen where as always, the kettle was simmering on the Aga. Helen made a pot of tea and they all sat around the kitchen table.

'How much does he know?' Jock directed the question at Helen as if Frank were not in the room.

'More than's good fer me, I reckon, an' I can speak fer meself.'

Over the course of the next hour everything was divulged. Her common sense and every ethical and virtuous fibre of her being was telling her it was wrong but Helen was warming to Jock's narrowboat plan if not quite as excited as he was. She had certainly made it perfectly clear there and then that there was no way in the world she was going to become a boatman's floozy. She would maintain a secretarial role and a catalogue of the goods. She insisted that additionally, there would be proper book-keeping for which she would be responsible. Various other ground rules were laid down and it was agreed that they would meet again at Kilby Wharf in the spring. For his part Frank wanted nothing to do with the business enterprise at all and he was anxious that his brother Ernie and niece Kate would not be complicit or compromised at all by any nefarious goings-on or black market trading. In fact, Frank was most insistent that his relatives should know nothing. He merely wanted all the 'unmentionables,' the dubiously acquired and stolen property removed from his barn as soon as possible. He did not, however, make any objection at Jock's insistence that he should retain a case of whisky and several ounces of St Bruno in return for the inconvenience he'd been put to.

It was well into the afternoon when Jock left. He had promised Frank that everything in the barn which shouldn't be there would be moved as soon as transport could be arranged. Frank had also been given the assurance that there would be no repercussions and that he would not be implicated at all. Even so, Helen could detect his concern as they drove to Kilby Bridge.

They arrived in time for tea. Helen was introduced to Frank's family and she immediately took to Kate. She'd be about eighteen, Helen thought. A pretty girl with blonde hair tied back in a plait. She was wearing similar clothes to those that until a few weeks ago Helen herself would have been wearing, the brown dungarees over a check shirt. As for Ernie, Frank's 'little' brother – he was enormous, six foot three inches and eighteen stone she estimated. But to listen to him he was softly spoken just like his elder brother and with identical mannerisms it was clear that Frank and Ernest were both from the same Black Country mould.

They all sat down to eat and with all plates scraped clean everyone had obviously enjoyed the meal. In part, this might have been due to the warm atmosphere of friendly, family, familiarity. The men remained at the table with a beer each discussing the hardships for the farming fraternity. Helen and Kate cleared away and whilst they were doing the dishes Helen learned that both Kate's mum, Victoria, and Franks' wife, Agnes, had been victims of an air raid. Helen couldn't understand why Frank had never mentioned it. Yes there was a discernible absence of a woman's touch about Frank's place but Helen had been too polite to ask. Now she knew and her filial affection for Frank was even greater.

With what remained of the daylight Helen's belongings were brought into the main house.

'Tha'll be stayin' 'ere tonight. We'll move you into t'cottage tomorrow.' It could have been Frank speaking. A simple statement, no debate, no point in offering any argument, that's the way it was. Helen gave Frank a hug and a kiss on the cheek. Having bidden his farewells, he was into the Austin and off into the twilight.

Chapter Eleven

While Helen and the Warings had been enjoying their evening, Jock had been charging about on the Ariel and eventually, from amongst his several contacts in the underworld he'd arranged a borrow an Austin K2/Y military ambulance. He had considered 'borrowing' a bus but decided it would be just a little conspicuous not to mention suspicious; a very late bus service pulling up in a farmyard? Maybe not! On the other hand an ambulance would be perfect. There were still plenty of them about; 'Katys' as they were affectionately known. People were used to seeing military vehicles on the road and nobody would question the presence of an ambulance in the dead of night. After all the 'Katy' had been the vehicle of choice by the SPIVs during an air-raid. They could loot a bombed-out building or a shop whilst everyone was below ground in the shelter. Anyone above ground would be thinking they were searching for casualties. Looted proceeds could be loaded into an ambulance without arousing suspicion and driven off with no-one the wiser. Sometimes when there was a 'big' job on, an accomplice, wearing a 'borrowed' ARP armband and helmet would lend further credibility to such opportunistic thieving.

With all decent respectable citizens tucked up in bed, Jock, aided and abetted by Ron, arrived at Frank's barn in the dead of night. Jock had 'killed' the engine in the lane and coasted into the farmyard. The invisibility of the camouflaged ambulance was also aided by its lights still being compliant with blackout regulations. The undercover operation went according to plan. They had not been disturbed and as far as they were aware had not been seen. But it had taken much longer than had been originally thought. In fact dawn was all but breaking when the ambulance pulled away fully loaded. A 'consideration' had been left in the barn for Frank. Jock dropped Ron off at home. He didn't want anyone apart from Helen to know where the cargo was to be stored. He promised to see his conductor at work later. They were on afternoons, the 658 Hinckley to Leicester route.

Emily Rose was moored at the Wharf. Jock had been hoping to get the boat loaded before daylight and he was now wondering whether leaving the transfer of cargo until later in the day was a better plan. He really needed some sleep before work that afternoon. Not turning up for work at this stage of the fledgling business would only set people wondering and was not an option. And he was not sure to what extent he could rely Ron on to keep quiet. He decided to drive back to the bomb site and park where his contact normally parked. It wouldn't appear unusual in the same spot where passers-by were accustomed to seeing it. OK there was a slight risk but it was worth it. What's more he had left Ron's motorbike there when he'd picked the ambulance up. That in itself could be awkward. If it was left there. He locked the ambulance, kicked the Ariel into life and went home and thence to work.

Chapter Twelve

After his shift during which he had made four round trips between Leicester and Hinckley Jock parked the bus at the depot changed out of his Midland Red uniform and into his old army blouson thinking it would be more befitting for the driver of a military vehicle. He cycled directly to where he'd left the ambulance. In his rucksack he had a torch, a pair of gloves, a flask of coffee and a couple of Spam sandwiches. The Austin 'Katy' sat there on the bomb site. Jock walked around it and from what he could see by torchlight, no one had interfered with it. He had a look in the back and was relieved to see that the cargo was intact. He extinguished his torch and went around to the driver's cab. As he was about to climb up he froze when the beam from another torch lit him up. He was aware of his heart racing and the beads of sweat forming on his forehead.

"What's going on here then?" came a voice he didn't recognise. Jock stepped down and turned in to the light. With the glare of the light directly in his eyes he couldn't make out who it was. The voice spoke again, this time undisguised.

'I knew you were scheming something yo' little Scot's bastard! If yo' think yo' can buy me off wi' a piss poor bribe, yo' can bloody well think again!' Now, Jock recognised the less than dulcet tones of his conductor, Ron. His heartrate decelerated and the butterflies in the pit of stomach settled.

'Och Ron, dinnae ye ever de that agin. I fair near shat masel'.'

Ron approached from out of the shadows and stood looking at Jock, with his head cocked to one side, a quizzical expression on his face which demanded Jock give him an explanation. Before he said anything, Jock's thought processes raced. He really didn't want to cut anyone else in. This was his and Helen's caper and besides which, the less the number of people who knew about it, the greater the chance of them getting away with it undetected.

'C'mon Jock, what yo' into here? I'm yo' mate. We cover each other's backs at work so why not now?' Jock was rapidly coming to the conclusion that he'd have to let Ron in. He could think of no alternative that would stop Ron from blabbing off to all and sundry.

'Och shit! OK, but ye'll gi' me yer promise; ye'll swear t' me the noo, that ye'll nae whisper a bloody word t' anyone!. If ye dae, it'll be the last thing ye ever dae!' Whilst Ron understood Jock's utterance he was visibly taken aback. Conceding as he might have been, Jock's delivery through clenched teeth and articulated 'sotto voce' was powerfully threatening. 'This is something big,' thought Ron.

'I give yo' me word Jock. I'll not let yo' down I promise – yo' can count on the word of a Brummie!'

'Alreet then c'mon get in the wagon!' The pair of them climbed into the cab of the ambulance and drove off.

It was well after midnight and there was very little traffic. On the way to the Wharf, Jock explained as little as he thought he could get away with. He admitted to himself that it would handy some extra muscle on hand not only for humping all the gear on board the *Emily Rose* but just in case any untoward 'interruptions' to their labours should require dissuasion by use of strong-arm tactics. Whereas Jock was no fighter, Ron had proved himself in that regard on more than a couple of occasions in the past

They drove into the yard at the rear of the Wharf and parked alongside the *Emily Rose* which had been conveniently berthed under some willow trees, the branches of which almost devoid of leaves now 'wept' over the boat providing cover. The night was generally cloudy with only the occasional break allowing the merest glimmer of moonlight. Jock stepped aboard the boat and began folding the cargo hold's canvas covering forward and out of the way. He stepped down into the hull and shone his torch forward. Arthur's last cargo had been fifteen tons of aggregate. Jock reckoned there was a hundredweight or so still scattered about the sole of the boat. He called Ron over and into the hold and handed him the broom and shovel that had been lashed to the frame of the cover intimating that he should fill the sacks. Jock went back to the ambulance and started unloading the various boxes and crates and stacking them on the quayside. Just as when they loaded the ambulance from the trailer in Frank's barn, dawn was breaking by the time they completed the transfer of goods from the Katy to the *Emily Rose*. The hold cover was replaced and secured. Ron was instructed to return the ambulance to the bomb site whilst Jock would remain in the boatman's quarters at the stern of the vessel 'to keep an eye on the cargo' he explained to Ron. He estimated that based on what he'd paid for it, the value of the boat now with the inclusion of the cargo had increased by as much as 500-fold. As soon as Ron had driven off, Jock returned to the hold, prised the lid off one of the wooden boxes and armed himself with the same German Luger pistol, just in case. Then, back in the cabin he checked the content of the fuel tank, and gratifyingly found it full. He fired up the Russell Newbery engine, cast his mooring lines off and hesitatingly edged the boat ahead and into the early morning and the middle of the cut to proceed up the arm towards the Ashby Canal.

Recalling the 'how hard can it be' thought that he'd had a couple of days earlier, it was now more a case of 'not as easy as it seems'. Jock had to admit that there was more to steering a seventy-two-foot narrowboat than one might imagine. It was as well it was still early with no one about to witness the haphazard progress he was making with the bow hitting the bank on one side then the other as he attempted to maintain a steady straight-line course. Jock was aware that this 'arm' joined the main Ashby Canal in just a few hundred yards where he would have to negotiate a tricky left-hand turn – tricky for the novice helmsman that is.

A few moments later he was passing the Lime Kilns, the pub where the whole narrowboat strategy was conceived. Even as he ran into the A5 bridge parapet, Jock remained convinced that it was a good plan. Since buying the boat, he had done some homework regarding where he was going, even so, he was pleased to see that there was a sketch map of the canal network in the cabin, obviously left there by Arthur. He was also thinking how he would get the 'business' up and running and start to make some money. But right at that moment, keeping the boat moving in a straight line was requiring all his concentration. 'How can just a small movement of the tiller make the bow veer off course so violently in one direction or the other?' he wondered. He was having jittery thoughts about what he might do if he encountered a boat coming towards him! One thing he was grateful for was the fact that on this his maiden voyage, he wouldn't have to contend with any locks since there are none on the Ashby Canal; it being the longest canal in Britain on one level. The plan was to head down the two miles or so to Marston Junction where the Ashby joined the Coventry Canal and then continue south past the Hawkesbury Junction with the Oxford Canal and after a further thirteen miles or so, find a spot to hole up near Rugby. One of the things Arthur had told him was that there are several small 'arms' which would afford an isolated spot and provide an opportunity to step ashore and get some provisions. Mindful, of not wishing to draw undue attention to himself or to the *Emily Rose*, he stuck to the speed limit of four miles-per-hour and gently chugged on, his confidence building. It was a chilly but not unpleasant autumnal day and Jock was quite enjoying his first canal cruising experience. Realising that he wouldn't be going back to the Midland Red, it occurred to him that whilst he could do Leicester to Hinckley and back four times in one shift, this one trip to somewhere near Leicester was going to take him more like four days.

He arrived at the Clifton Arm just passed Rugby during the early part of the afternoon and managed to 'hide' the boat a short way into the arm. He put out a bow and a stern line and all without any difficulty or disaster. He decided he'd worry about getting out of the arm when the time came next morning. It had been quite a while since he'd finished the coffee and the Spam sandwiches were long gone. So Jock went walkabout to see what provisions he might procure.

He returned some time later. Daylight was fading and he decided to light the small stove in the cabin. He made himself comfortable and the cabin was soon warm and snug. He set about 'fleshing out' the bones of his plans whilst he ate the meagre provisions he'd been able to procure. Ultimately he wanted to find somewhere which he could use as a base. Ideally somewhere near to familiar territory and where he could keep in touch with those members of the underground with whom he had fairly regular dealings. Not too far from a main road and a pub would be handy as well. He'd also need to be somewhere not too distant from Helen's location wherever that was, somewhere near Kilby he seemed to remember she'd said. He studied the sketch map and considered a location near Wigston to the south of Leicester as a possibility. It was then that his pulse started to race as he saw the numerous obstacles he would have to overcome to get there. The following and subsequent days would present many challenges the first of which would be the Hillmorton locks, reputedly the busiest flight of locks on the entire canal network. Jock began to worry how he would cope, indeed whether he would cope at all singlehandedly. Arthur had talked him through the locking procedure and now he wished he'd paid more attention. Then if he managed to get beyond Hillmorton there were even greater challenges presenting themselves after the Braunston turn. He would have to contend with six locks, and a tunnel on his way to the Grand Union Leicester Line junction at Long Buckby. He decided there and then albeit with trepidation that if he came through these challenges on day two of his boating career he would celebrate the achievement by cracking open a bottle of scotch from 'the stores'. He sat there mentally rehearsing the locking procedures and eventually drifted off the sleep.

When he awoke, Jock checked his pocket watch. Six-thirty-five. He stuck his head out of the cabin. It was still dark and it was drizzling.

'I've a long way tae go an' it willnae be easy so let's be at it Jock laddie!' he said by way of a self-motivational speech. He stepped ashore to untie his mooring lines then decided he needed to take a leak. Buttoning up his fly he noticed that even in this slight early morning breeze the boat had been blown away from the bank. 'Bugger!' he muttered. It needed the deployment of every ounce of strength he could muster to pull the boat sufficiently close to the bank to allow him to jump on. He went below to fire up the Russell Newbery. It took several attempts, with Jock cranking like crazy before the engine finally caught. He returned to the tiller and saw to his horror that the wind had now blown him some considerable distance in the wrong direction. He gingerly selected 'astern' and after a while the boat responded and began to move stern first towards the main Oxford canal. Completely misjudging the turn and by his failure to account for the windage, he succeeded, very unsuccessfully, in running the stern of the *Emily Rose* up the opposite bank with the bow caught on the corner he was attempting to get round. Here they were, stuck and completely blocking the canal. He put the engine in neutral and hesitantly crept forward along the very narrow gunwale and using the bargepole and exerting an enormous effort coupled with a great deal of cursing and swearing he managed to push the bow round to face the desired direction of travel. He crept back to the steering platform, put the engine into gear and managed to get underway.

'No' the best start tae the day,' Jock thought. His blouson was soaked and he was less than impressed. He peered ahead into the gloom and could just make out the first of the Hillmorton locks in the distance and there didn't appear to be any other traffic, which was an enormous relief for Jock and his mood lightened.

'Well would ye look at that. A piece o' luck if ever I needed wan!' he spoke out loudly. Clearly the last boat to use the lock had been going towards Hawkesbury and left it full. Jock engaged neutral as he recalled Arthur's instruction and the boat glided slowly into the lock barely touching the side and gently nudging the gate at the far end before coming to a halt. Jock hopped onto the side of the lock and closed the gate behind the boat. Before doing anything else he sat down and reflected on the previous forty minutes or so.

'Lessons to be learned,' he thought. He made mental notes: 'Get some proper wet-weather kit, be aware o' the wind, dinnae untie the boat then decide tae take a piss, and gi' her some wellie in reverse'. He then talked himself through the lock routine which he proceeded to execute perfectly.

The next two locks were equally simple with no problems and having cleared the Hillmorton hurdle Jock congratulated himself and despite every stitch of clothing he had on being thoroughly wet through he was rather pleased with his efforts and began enjoying the day.

As he rounded the Braunston turn, Jock could see signs of civilisation on the left bank and also a little further ahead on the right after the London Road bridge. He decided he would stop and like an expert he drew into the bank, gave the engine a kick astern and stepped ashore neatly looping the stern line around a bollard as he did so. The bow then drifted into the bank and he made his bow line fast.

At a small shop he was able to get some supplies including some rationed goods which after a bit of bartering, were exchanged for some cigarettes and a couple of bottles from the 'stores'. Noticing the drenched state he was in, the shopkeeper offered him a second-hand pair of yellow oilskin trousers and jacket in return for a further consideration from *Emily Rose*'s bountiful hold. The deal was readily agreed. Jock also took on some fresh water and bucket of coal for the stove. The diesel fuel tank was still all but full; the engine seemingly having hardly used much fuel at all. He sat on board and made himself a sandwich and a cup of tea before restarting the engine, casting off and proceeding down to the six Braunston locks.

There were several other boats passing up and down which in some respects was fortunate for Jock. Unlike the Hillmorton single locks, the Braunston locks were doubles and whereas a boat would lie nice and comfortably in a single lock without the need for lines ashore, this was not the case in a double. However, looking the part in his newly acquired yellow oilskins, other boatmen with their crews assumed Jock to be one of them and readily assisted him with his warps and with the lock paddles and gates. Even so it took a considerable amount of time to work through the locks and into the tunnel. The tunnel was a completely 'out of this world experience' for Jock. At nearly two miles long *Emily Rose* was in the eerie darkness for a good half-an-hour. Luckily Jock had a boat to follow. Emerging eventually into daylight again Jock checked his pocket watch. With the rain and drizzle it hadn't really got light all day and now it would soon be properly dark. He decided to moor for the night at Norton Junction. Just a little way ahead at Long Buckby Wharf he could see what looked like a pub where the Watling Street crossed the canal. Mindful that it was only the previous day when he had passed under the Watling Street by the Lime Kilns he decided that he would take his celebratory drink in the pub, the New Inn.

This decision proved to be beneficial in several respects. Not only was it a grand pub with good beer and a roaring fire, he was made most welcome. He managed to dry out his still damp clothes, he won ten shillings playing dominoes with some the locals who then turned out to be good customers for some of Jock's comestible cargo; a profitable evening all round. As part of the deal with his partner he managed to keep a record of what he'd sold and bartered since the beginning of his voyage. He hoped Helen would be impressed. He hadn't given Ron a second thought since he drove away in the ambulance the previous day.

Chapter Thirteen

Of all the seasons on the farm, Frank liked the winter the least. Of all the months in the winter Frank disliked November the most. It had been a gruelling day, raining, the ground getting churned up, but he and the lad had finally managed to get the cattle into the sheds. He had just sat down with his pipe and a drop of hard stuff. He thought he'd earned it. The peace and tranquillity were broken by a most insistent knock at the door.

'Who the bloody 'ell is that at this time o' night?' he wondered. His bones were aching as he heaved himself out of his armchair by the fire. 'Cor, I'm getting old,' he thought.

He opened the door and was most surprised to see Gordon Almey, the village constable, standing there with another bloke he didn't recognise at all.

'Ow do Frank. This 'ere's Detective Sergeant Dave Hollis, Frank. Can we come in, there's a few questions the Sergeant'd like to ask if that's OK?'

' Course, c'mon in out o' t'cold. Would you like a drop of…?' Gordon hushed him.

'You know I would Frank but best not whilst Sergeant's 'ere.' They moved into Frank's sitting room. Gordon stood with his backside to the fire, helmet under his arm. The

Detective had picked up the Macallan bottle and was examining it.

'Do you mind telling me how you came by this whisky?'the Detective asked.

'It were given to me by the land-army girl who used t' work for us.' Frank replied.

'And where I wonder, did she get it from?'

'I reckon 'er 'usband got it.' Frank was fully aware that Gordon suspected that he was not quite telling the whole truth, but the last thing Frank wanted was to get Helen into trouble and Gordon was not one to interfere.

'What was her name, your land-army girl?' Frank felt obliged to tell him.

'And where can I locate her?' Frank did not feel inclined to tell him.

'I don't know. She got in t' family way and couldn't work for me anymore and she moved away at the end of the summer.' Then completely out of the blue,

'I'm arresting you on suspicion of handling stolen goods,' announced the Detective, who proceeded to caution Frank.

'Best get your coat,' said Gordon.

Detective Hollis had put the Macallan bottle in his coat pocket. 'Evidence,' he explained.

Hollis bundled Frank into the back of the police Ford Anglia and got in beside him. PC Almey was driving.

After some two hours of questioning during which Frank managed to evade all the incriminating questions he was released without charge although the 'evidence' wasn't returned to him. Gordon, who'd known Frank for years, and who was renowned and respected by everyone locally for interpreting and upholding the law in a common sense fashion, drove Frank back to the farm.

'They know there's summat going on Frank. I just hope you're not involved nor that girl o' yours.'

'Thanks Gordon. I've told you all I can.' Frank said sincerely and in all honesty, since he'd told the police all he could without landing Helen and Jock in a whole lot of bother or even jail perhaps. He certainly wasn't about to start telling them any more than he already had. Frank returned to his sitting room. There were just a few glowing embers left in the fireplace and happily, whilst the bottle may have been confiscated, the glass he'd poured before the arrival of the police was still on the table virtually untouched.

Next morning the farm lad, Frank's labourer, turned up, punctual as ever, although 6 am was an ungodly hour especially on a wet, bleak November morning. Frank gave him his instructions.

'If anyone comes looking for me, yo' ain't seen me, OK? Yo' don't know where I've gone and yo' don't know when I'll be back, OK?' He was at pains to emphasise the importance of this particular order. The lad was slightly puzzled but he knew how to do as he was told.

'That's ok, Mr Waring. Yo' can trust me'. And, as he drove off in the Austin, Frank knew he could too.

Frank made sure he wasn't followed and took a bit of a circuitous route through various villages just to be sure. When he arrived at Ernest's farm he hid the car behind a barn. Ernie came out to meet him.

'Eh up Frank, where's t' fire?'

'Where's Helen? It's urgent.' They went inside and Frank told him about the previous evening's visit.

'I need to speak to Helen.' Frank was clearly worried.

'She's not involved, is she?' questioned Ernie.

'I'd rather not tell yo' owt Ernie. What yo' don't know can't hurt yo'.' Ernie accepted this explanation although he was somewhat disturbed by it.

Frank drove the quarter mile to Helen's cottage and Frank gave her the details as far as he knew of what the police knew. Helen was distressed that Frank had been arrested especially since it was as a result of him doing her a favour in the first place. After a while, a cup of tea, and a slice of toast with home-baked bread and jam, the situation had calmed down although an uneasy tension remained. Helen mentioned that she was expecting Jock to get in touch with her within a few days and that she would sort matters out with him. She didn't want Frank worrying unnecessarily.

Clearly unhappy with the situation and Helen's involvement he got up to leave.

'Just be careful Helen. That Jock's a wrong 'un. He's a villain and no mistake. If owt happened to yo' I dunno what I'd do'.

As Frank left, the anxiety could be detected in his demeanour. Helen had tears in her eyes. She was upset and no mistake.

Chapter Fourteen

On the voyage so far Jock had been reliant on the sketch map of the canal system that presumably, the previous owner of *Emily Rose* Arthur, had prepared. Whilst he was moored at Norton Junction Jock was able to buy a rather more detailed chart of the canal going north towards Leicester. Before setting off he studied it carefully. Knowing now, albeit with just a couple of days' experience, what his rate of progress was likely to be it was important that he could plan his overnight stops, recognise where not to stop, and know where he could get supplies.

Yesterday's rain had cleared up but the skies were still overcast. Jock had checked the engine; being a bus driver he was well aware just how these routine matters were important. And, as if by way of a thank you, the Russell Newbery started at the first time of asking. Having noted how the professional boatmen looped their mooring warps around the bollards, Jock too could now merely slip his lines without having to step ashore to do so. With no locks to contend with initially he'd estimated that he could reach the first major obstacles of the day within a couple of hours of plain sailing. Ever mindful of what his objectives were Jock was constantly aware of the surrounding countryside through which he was passing. Making mental notes of places where he could secretly liaise with potential clients or drop stuff off for actual customers was critical to the covert running of the business. As he guided *Emily Rose* through bridge Number 3, Ball's Bridge, he noted its proximity to the main London Road, the A5, yet in the middle of nowhere. A possibility? Maybe. The chart also told him just how close the canal on this stretch ran to the railway line. As if to emphasis the fact, an express passenger train came seemingly out of nowhere and rushed across bridge Number 5A over the canal on its way to London.

Within minutes of this piece of excitement Jock had reached the Watford flight of locks. There were a couple of boats ahead of him working their way through the flight and not having experienced a 'flight' before Jock took the sensible decision to observe how it should be approached and came alongside a waiting mooring. He walked up the towpath and watched with interest. The whole operation was directed by the lockkeeper who, upon seeing Jock and noticing the *Emily Rose* below the flight, approached him and had a word. Instantly Jock was overcome with misgivings. He hadn't reckoned on encountering any form of officialdom. Clearly the lockkeeper was an official.

'Would he keep a record, would he want to know about the cargo, would he want to inspect a licence or a manifest?' These and many other doubts precipitated Jock into a flat spin. 'C'mon, pull yersel' togither man. Dinnae panic or you'll gi' the game away!' he urged himself.

Having watched the boats ahead work the flight under the scrutiny of and with the assistance of the lockkeeper Jock had noted how, after Bottom Lock, Number 1, those that followed were akin to a staircase where two locks were connected in the middle by a shared gate. With the lockkeeper now beckoning to him it was his turn. 'I must keep calm,' he was telling himself. And calm he was. He glided into Number 2 and by the time he cleared Top Lock Number 7 he was wondering what he'd been worrying about. 'Nae bother!' he thought. He looked back and gave the lockkeeper a wave. The lockkeeper didn't wave back or otherwise acknowledge. To Jock's consternation he seemed to be making an entry into a small notebook.

Wanting to put some distance between himself and the keeper of the Watford Locks he nudged the throttle forward and by the time he'd cleared the Kilsby Road bridge, Number 8, he eased *Emily Rose* into the bank and put the kettle on.

Looking at his chart the prospect of a night in the wilderness had absolutely no appeal to Jock and he resolved to push on through the Crick Tunnel to bridge Number 11, remote enough but sufficiently close to civilisation. The boats that had been ahead of him at the Watford Locks would be well ahead by now he reasoned. Therefore he should be able to make it before dark. There was precious little daylight left when he entered the tunnel. It was unbelievably damp presumably from the recent rain which was now seeping through the tunnel's brickwork. In fact such was the amount of water dripping from the roof he eased the engine down to tick-over speed and quickly retrieved his oilskin jacket from the cabin. Again he witnessed the ghostly, nightmarish unease that he had felt during his first tunnel experience at Braunston. However this tunnel was shorter by almost two-thirds of a mile and just beyond the tunnel parapet was his planned overnight stop. There was no light at the end of the tunnel when *Emily Rose* emerged. Jock 'killed' the engine and coasted into the bank where he had to improvise some iron stakes shoved into the ground as makeshift bollards around which to loop his mooring warps. He'd been wondering what they were for. Safely secured, he lit the stove and prepared a stew of potatoes and carrots that he had picked up at Long Buckby; days ago, for so it seemed.

Recharged by his hot food, Jock picked up his torch and lit his way across the field towards the lights in the distance. His hopes were realised when he saw the sign gently swinging beneath the thatch of a stone-built coaching inn. The Red Lion. Jock could not recall a more welcoming sight since the troop ship that brought him back from the Gold Coast. He bought a pint and sat by the fire thinking about his army days and the humble beginnings of his black market racket and the manner in which it had developed and might continue so to do.

Jock stayed in the pub until closing time. What else was there to do? He'd been enjoying some banter with a few of the locals and he'd taken rather a fancy to the barmaid. So it was with more than several pints and a few tots inside him his return to the boat went off on a couple of tangents and took a few wayward turns before he was back aboard.

The following morning when he ventured out of the cabin he was greeted by a brighter day with maybe even a promise of some sunshine. There was a small gathering of men on the towpath.

'Who the…., what the…?' then he remembered. None-too-discreetly he'd vocally advertised his wares in the pub last night and here were his customers.

'This is too easy,' Jock thought. He slipped the cover back on the hold just enough to gain entry and proceeded to fulfil the orders as they were relayed to him. He asked one of the locals to deliver a pair of stockings to the barmaid, 'Wi Jock's compliments!' he pronounced with a big grin.

He had a bit of a stocktake and noted eight bottles of whisky, six of gin, a case of French wine, 1000 cigarettes and a Rolex watch into the 'goods sold' column of the exercise book he now had for the purpose. At the bottom of the daily income column he entered a total of £192/10/6. Almost ten times the average weekly wage in just half-an-hour. He didn't make a note of the nylons!

He refastened the cover of his 'warehouse' and got underway. The plan for the day, given the success of the previous day, was to make the twenty-seven miles or so to North Kilworth. Eminently feasible since there were no locks to impede his progress. It wasn't long into the trip that he began to realise why there were no locks. Jock had always understood that canals, as distinct from rivers, were fairly straight line waterways. This, the Leicester Line of the Grand Union twisted and turned all over the place following the natural contours of the countryside.

'Still, nae matter' thought Jock. The sun was shining and the late autumn countryside with the last of the leaves in all shades of gold and russet clinging to the trees was beautiful.

'Grand,' he said. 'Ye' can stick yer bloody North Africa!' He'd reached the Welford Junction by mid-afternoon but decided it might prove to be more lucrative to go a little further. According to his chart, bridge Number 45 carried the road between two villages. North Kilworth to the west and Husbands Bosworth to the east.

'If I can find a pub in both villages there's potential to double the take,' he reasoned.

As he approached North Kilworth Wharf he could see several narrowboats moored on either bank of the canal. He manoeuvred *Emily Rose* into a space between two other similar sized boats that didn't look as if they were working boats or even occupied, never mind going anywhere soon. From the bridge *Emily Rose* would appear to be just another boat. Jock heated up and finished the leftover potato and carrot stew and after tossing a coin, went to the bridge and took the westerly direction towards North Kilworth. It was a good mile or so but when he arrived Jock found the White

Lion on the main road and it was open. The next couple of hours followed the pattern of the previous evening in The Red Lion; drinking, socialising, womanising, and sowing the seeds for a few surreptitious sales. Noticing the time on his pocket watch he bade his farewells with a 'Might see you in the morning then?' and made his way back towards the bridge over the canal with his thumb out. He thought that by wearing his army blouson as he was a car might take pity and give an ex-serviceman a lift. No such luck! It was almost forty minutes after leaving the White Lion that he arrived with a raging thirst at The Bell, a rather grand looking Georgian fronted inn. After downing a couple of pints in rapid order Jock settled to his normal pace and the routine that was becoming established.

At closing time, he was fortunate enough to get a lift with a fellow on his BSA Bantam; not quite Ron's Ariel but better than walking.

'Bugger!' Jock cursed. 'Bloody Ron. I'd forgotten all aboot 'im. He'll be wantin' ma guts fur garters.' And it was that prompt from his guilty conscience that was the cause of a fitful night's sleep; nothing at all to do with his indigestion.

The queue by *Emily Rose* the next morning was rather disappointing given that Jock had made twice the effort. Even so when he did his book-keeping he was able to enter £156/4s/9d.

'At this rate' he thought, 'I'll be runnin' oot ay stock… I' better see whit I can de aboot it.'

With the 'shop' closed he shoved off and motored towards Foxton through the shorter half-mile or so Husbands Bosworth tunnel and the rural countryside. He knew that the Foxton flight of locks was a big deal but nothing had prepared him for what he saw ahead as he cleared bridge Number 60; the magnificent sight of ten locks in two staircases of five each. To work his way through here even with the guidance and assistance of the lockkeeper was going to take the rest of the day.

The only other traffic Jock could see was the narrowboat ascending the flight towards him. This was good news. It meant that *Emily Rose* would have every lock made ready without having to fill them first. What's more, Jock had decided that descending was much more straightforward than going up. As the *Damselfly* came through Foxton Top Lock, Number 8 on the Leicester Line, Jock was prepared, waiting for the lockkeeper's acknowledgement which was readily forthcoming. The next three hours were spent slowly gliding down to Bottom Lock number 17. The passage had not been quite without incident. As *Emily Rose* slid into lock number 12, Jock could see another boat ahead of him in the passing pound. He hadn't been expecting this. The *Mayfly*, judging by the name and the livery, was obviously the sister boat to *Damselfly* and she was waiting to continue up as soon as Jock had descended through number 12 and into the pound. There was some confusion as to which side he should pass on. *Mayfly*, laden to gunnels with coal by the look of it was loitering in the centre of the pound and with both skippers anxious to make progress, there was something of a 'coming together'; just a slight grazing of each boat's starboard sides, neither having bothered to deploy their fenders. On the side of the pound the lockkeeper threw his arms in the air and started gesticulating and hurling abuse at one or both of them not that Jock could hear what was being hurled. Jock shouted back anyway, 'Worse things happen at sea!'

The *Mayfly* disappeared into lock Number 12 and *Emily Rose* manoeuvred comfortably into lock Number 13 and the respective gates were closed behind them with their paddles lowered. Lock Numbers 14,15,16 presented no difficulty and leaving 16 he cleared bridge Number 61 and into the final lock, Foxton Bottom Number 17. A second lockkeeper opened the gate and directed Jock over to the right indicating that he should tie up and that there was some kind of formality that required to be dispensed with. 'Was this going to be trouble?' Jock wondered. The only formality Jock was interested in could be dealt with inside the Foxton Locks Inn, the pub outside which he had just tied up. The lockkeeper approached.

'Private or commercial?' he enquired. The question threw Jock off-balance.

'Private,' Jock responded confidently. The lockkeeper picked up some kind of yardstick that had been leaning against the wall at one end of the pub building, an office presumably. He then placed his measuring stick vertically against the hull of *Emily Rose*.

'You're down seven inches.' He consulted a card which he withdrew from his inside pocket.

'That'll be fourteen shillings and seven pence please.'

Jock was taken aback. 'Whit for? he demanded.

'Toll, you're seven inches down, that's seven tons you're carrying at two-and-a-penny a ton, as well you know. Don't think you can fool me with your foreign accent.'

Sometimes Jock's Scots dialect bordered on unintelligible.

He didn't need more than a few seconds to realise that any argument would be futile and only display his ignorance of such canal-related matters. Thinking again, he decided to give it a go anyway and offer a bribe.

'Would ye nae prefer a bottle ay Glenmorangie?" To Jock's surprise that was indeed the lockkeeper's preference and they both disappeared into the pub.

Chapter Fifteen

Just before Christmas of 1945 Frank came to visit Helen. She was delighted to see him and they spent hours sitting and chatting in Ernie's tied cottage which she had transformed into her home. It was warm and comfortable and one the happiest times in several months for both of them until Frank broke the news which had been the main purpose of his visit.

'I don't often bother wi' it, but last week I got a copy of the local paper 'cos I were a-looking fer an advert fer some paint I needed. I 'ad a glance though the obituary column and the name Robinson fair jumped off the page. I di'n't know if you'd 'ave 'ad the news. It were your mam Helen. I'm very sorry.' There followed an uneasy pause. Frank wasn't sure whether to expect tears, a lapse into a lamentable grieving or what. One could never predict how Helen would react. Since Ken had left it was not often in Frank's experience at least, that Helen exhibited any emotion at all neither joyful nor woeful. After several more minutes devoid of any release of feeling she looked at Frank in such a way as to bring a lump to his throat.

'Would you like another cup of tea?' Nothing more was ever mentioned about Liz's demise.

Christmas Day at Ernie's farm proved to be a genial

celebration with much merrymaking and good cheer. Kate, with Helen's assistance, had prepared a magnificent feast the likes of which had not been enjoyed since before the war. Frank and Ernest were as happy as their 'pigs in muck'. Helen was excused from clearing away given the proximity to her 'due' date but once it was done they sat to open their few gifts. Attention was then focussed on the wireless and the King's Christmas message. Neither Frank nor Ernie were particularly impressed by the King's reference to world peace having become a reality but there seemed to be a general consensus of accord with his statement that 'much of great price had been given up to attain victory.' But was that which had been saved really beyond value? Whatever! With the atmosphere getting a bit thick with Frank's pipe smoke mingling with the pollution from Ernie's cigar of Churchillian proportions, Kate and Helen went for a walk in what remained of the daylight leaving the men to their port. When the girls returned the men were both asleep snoring away in their armchairs and the fire almost out for the want of being tended.

When he next visited, between Boxing Day and New Year's Eve, Frank agreed to drive Helen to visit Mabel and Albert. She hadn't seen them since the episode with Ken and whilst she had convinced Frank that she merely wanted to wish them seasonal greetings, she was curious to learn whether or not they had received any news of their son; her absentee husband. All they could say was that they had received a Christmas card with a postmark from somewhere in Scotland. Albert suggested that he'd gone back to Fort George. After all, he reasoned, Ken knew people there from when he was in the army.

At the beginning of January Helen went into labour. She managed to get to the big house where Kate did whatever she could whilst Ernie drove off to fetch the midwife. The weather was bitterly cold with wintery showers being blown in on a fierce north-easterly wind. Even so he had managed to get word to Frank and then on to collect Nurse Holmes. When they got back to the farm all was going well according to Kate. Frank must have walked several miles pacing up and down in the kitchen as if he was the expectant father. Then after almost twelve hours the men heard the cries of a new-born baby from the spare room. Kate came rushing downstairs besides herself in unbridled delight,

'It's a boy! A beautiful bonny boy!' she announced. According to the midwife the birth had been quite straightforward with no complications and mother and baby were both absolutely fine. Ernie produced two bottles of Everards' finest and the brothers took great pleasure in 'wetting the baby's head'. A couple of days later, with her adopted family all proudly gathered around the bed and the crib, Frank stopped making cooing noises long enough to ask, 'ave ye decided on 'is name?"

'His name is Ben. Benjamin Robert Blake,' Helen announced.

At Helen's request Frank called on Albert and Mabel to let them know of the birth. Mabel became quite animated on hearing the news. Her delight was pure unabashed joyfulness, and she danced into the kitchen to put the kettle on. Albert's approval was restricted to a grin.

'Well fancy that! Me, a bloody grandad!'

After much discussion Albert decided that Ken, as the father of the new-born, should be informed. He wrote a letter and addressed it more in hope than expectation *to Sergeant Kenneth Blake, c/o Seaforth Highlanders, Fort George, Scotland.* Since seeing Helen just after Christmas he had thought a lot about his son's whereabouts. The more he thought, the more he was convinced that Ken would have gone back to the army. Surely his letter would be delivered.

Chapter Sixteen

Ken was both incensed and revolted. He couldn't bring himself to even think about how he and his pregnant wife had actually stayed in a house whilst there were two dead, and in the heat of the summer sun, decomposing bodies upstairs. Being a SPIV, a black marketeer was one thing. Being an accessory to a double murder was something altogether far far more serious. The burden of guilt was weighing heavily. He was guilty so many offences throughout his army career from misdemeanours to felonious transgression of army regulations; from aiding and abetting the Scotsman to downright villainy, whilst all the time putting on a respectable front. He was now deeply ashamed of the way in which he'd treated his wife. The fact that his iniquitous and illegal enterprise looked as though it would disappear down the toilet was no excuse and bore no justification for the despicable hellishness to which he had subjected Helen. It would be entirely understandable If she never wanted to see him again. Likewise his parents. He had let them down so terribly badly.

The self-condemnation and remorseful contrition he was now experiencing were only a part of the reasons he'd taken the spur-of-the-moment decision to leave. Or so he was trying to convince himself; nothing to do with having become an accessory to murder, to having committed the misappropriation of government property, theft, larceny, fraud, deception and domestic abuse; and on the charge sheet that would just be for starters. Oh no! Ken would be the last to admit that the characteristics he was now displaying were nothing more or less than those of a coward. 'If only they understood,' mused Ken. 'When my ship comes in, I'll be in a position to look after everyone and we'll want for nothing.'

On the night he had left, he'd caught the first northbound train at Leicester London Road and however many changes he had to make his intention had always been to get to the Highlands, out of the way where no one could find him. After two days during which he'd had precious little sleep he was at Edinburgh's Waverley Station. There were soldiers from one or other Highland Regiment on the concourse and he made a few enquiries of them as a result of which he bought a ticket to Comrie via Kirkcaldy and Perth. Cultybraggan Camp Number 21, sometimes known as the 'Black Camp of the North' had been nothing more than a name to him when he was at Fort George. Now apparently, according to the soldiers with whom he'd been speaking, it was a German Prisoner of War camp where Officers from the SS, Wehrmacht and Luftwaffe were incarcerated. Ken thought that unless the army had found him out, his record was unblemished and he'd be allowed to sign up for a further tour of duty, ideally as a guard at Camp 21.

On arrival at Comrie Station, Ken took a taxi to Cultybraggan and after the commanding officer had confirmed his record with Fort George and verified who Sergeant Kenneth Blake was Ken was permitted to sign up for the duration. It was anticipated that the Camp would close in 1948 when the Germans would be repatriated. As a welcome bonus he wasn't expecting he was able to retain his rank. Then, issued with a new uniform, Ken was shown to his quarters; his home for the next couple of years or so. This thought Ken, is my penitence. Right at that moment he didn't care about the contents of the spare room or the outhouse. He didn't care about his family. He did care about himself and only himself.

Sergeant Blake soon settled into a routine; an army routine, the kind of routine with which he was familiar. For Ken it was a form of escapism. On his days off he could wander into the Aberuchill hills and enjoy the solitude and the grandeur of the spectacular Highland scenery. The memory and reality of the previous couple of months was fading. He could sleep at night. He'd made new friends, even with some of the German prisoners who were looked after more in the manner of guests at a holiday camp than POWs.

Then there was a letter. Once a week a dispatch rider delivered mail, orders, bulletins, notices and whatever else from Fort George. 'Sergeant Kenneth Blake, c/o Seaforth Highlanders, Fort George, Scotland'. He took the letter to his quarters. He'd instantly recognised the handwriting on the envelope as his father's and was in two minds as to whether or not to open it. This instant contact with the past was too much. He tossed his Glengarry onto the bed and all the recent horror came flooding back. He opened the letter and what he read went some way to stemming the flow of all that which up until that moment had been drifting into oblivion. He had a son.

With trembling hands he took the whisky bottle from his locker and poured a generous draught into a glass which he drained in one swallow. He poured a second measure. Ken was unsure about the feeling this news had stirred in him. Was it guilt or shame? Was it pride or love? Was he capable of moral sensibility, of tender emotionalism? He drained the bottle and lay back on the bed.

The following day, having given the situation a great deal of thought he sat down with pen and paper. In his distinctive hand he wrote a reply to his parents.

Some four weeks after writing, a letter addressed to Albert in the unmistakeable 'copperplate' script of his son arrived.

Dear Mam and Dad

I'm sorry not to have been in touch especially after the way I took off leaving my new wife in the lurch and in the family way as well. I had my reasons as I know you'll realise and one day I might tell you all about it. Let's just say for now that I was in a bit of trouble and just needed to get away. I've signed on again and the army life suits me well enough and I've got some good mates. I'm in good health and I hope you both are.

Thanks for letting me know about my new son, Ben. Congratulations on becoming grandparents. Does he look anything like me? I'll apply for some compassionate leave and come down to visit.

That's all for now
Your son
Ken

Albert was flabbergasted! Not a word about Helen. Did he not care? Did he not want to know how she was, where she was, how she was coping, what she was doing for money?

Clearly not. Albert was extremely vexed that his son should have turned out like this.

With the news of the birth of his son, Ken had been given special dispensation for leave of absence to visit his family but he had no intention of doing any such thing. He'd received word, the word he'd been waiting for since returning from the war. His share of an extremely valuable 'consignment' had finally reached the UK and the 'heat' had cooled to the extent that he could now take delivery. Ken travelled south but rather than show up anywhere where he might be recognised, even with the beard he had grown, he took a room at The Old Greyhound, an inn, in a village to the south east of Leicester. The landlord was a most genial fellow, ruddy faced and portly. He introduced himself as George and insisted on showing Ken around his establishment.

'The oldest building in Great Glen,' Ken was informed. He was also shown the stables and the blacksmiths shop next door. Returning to the pub, Ken asked about the three greyhounds heads on the pub sign. This was his half-hearted gesture of showing some interest.

'Ah yes, it were the coat of arms of the Nele family who were t' Lords o' Manor back in sixteenth century.' Then in the best Italian accent that a Midlands' dialect could muster,

'Ancora una volta con sentimento – Courage, Vigilance, Fidelity.'

'Once more with feeling? Sod that! I've still got a chance with courage and vigilance, but I've buggered the third!' thought Ken.

After he'd settled in and had a meal he walked up towards St Cuthbert's church and found a telephone kiosk. He made a couple of calls and eventually got to speak to the right contact. It was arranged that his crate would be delivered by army transport to The Old Greyhound in Great Glen near Leicester. And two days later it was. Things were working out for Ken. Those years ducking and diving between The Gold Coast and various European theatres had certainly been profitable and now the profit had been delivered. It took Ken, George and the two squaddies from the van to lift and carry it.

'Struth, what yo' got in 'ere then, the crown jewels?'

'Something like that!' Ken replied with a laugh. His ship had just come in. The goose had laid the golden egg at last.

Later over a couple of pints, Ken took George into his

confidence although with a very spurious description of the contents of the crate. He asked George if he'd be so kind as to allow Ken to leave his crate at the pub for safekeeping because he had to return to Scotland. He would be back to collect it after a few days. George was only too happy to oblige

'I'll lock it in one o' t' stables. It'll be perfectly safe and secure in there don't you be a-worryin'.'

The next day Ken rallied some assistance and the crate was taken into one of the stables. The door was locked and bolted. George gave him a lift to Leicester and Ken returned to Cultybraggan Camp.

Chapter Seventeen

Despite her erstwhile husband having abandoned her Helen and baby Ben were becoming accustomed to each other and the daily round that they had established. Ernest, or Uncle Ernie, as he was now referred to, and Aunty Kate provided all that mother and baby needed and more. It really was 'home sweet home'. The absentee father was not so much of a problem either since Frank on his almost daily visits was more than happy to assume the role. They could not have been in a better more loving place. On Sundays either Frank or Ernie would drive over to pick up Albert and Mabel and lunch would be served in the big farmhouse kitchen. For Helen this was family life at its best even though her 'family' with the one small exception were all 'adopted'.

Spring of 1946 was late. There were unseasonal snow-falls and life on the farm became a little stressful as the seasonal work got behind schedule. Helen was also feeling stressed with postnatal depression maybe. She was lonely yet not isolated notwithstanding all the attention she and Ben received from Kate. She needed to get out, even if only to push Ben around the farmyard in the second-hand 'Silver Cross' perambulator that Frank had supplied. A rare treat came on the Whitsun weekend June 9th, when the sun shone. A trip was arranged and Ben was introduced to some of his actual relatives. Aunty Rosemary, and Uncles John, Charlie, Sid and Frank. They'd all made the effort to meet their sister and new nephew. Blankets were spread on the grass by the bandstand in Hollycroft Park, and everyone had an enjoyable time with a splendid picnic. Ben's reaction to the local brass band's performance kept everyone amused and one or two of his poses were captured by Uncle Sid on his Box Brownie camera. Helen wondered whether she could get him maybe a Leica for his birthday. And so for the Blakes and the Warings life went on.

For Mr Jock McClean, his meeting with Fred the lock-keeper at Foxton proved to be fortuitous. They had become firm friends and drinking pals. Fred's moral principles, or, more accurately the lack of, were as unscrupulous as Jock's. Opportunism was his adage. Fred was acquainted with most of the locals and he knew by name all the boatmen and their families that worked their way up and down the canal. Their itinerant lifestyle was hard and healthy and the rewards were not great. It was therefore not unreasonable for a boatman to appreciate a perk or a bargain every now and then. Fred had been working for the canal company since he left school and as one of the keepers of the Foxton Locks since before the war. Leaning on the bar of an evening Fred would often regale Jock with his tales of woe; competition from the burgeoning railway system, the increase in road transport detrimentally affecting commercial traffic on the cut, the Grand Union line between London and the Midlands silting up. The arrival of Jock, and more particularly, the arrival of *Emily Rose* and her cargo were especially welcome.

The *Emily Rose* remained moored outside the Foxton Locks Inn for the winter. Occasionally the canal froze, but Jock had a ready supply of fuel for his stove which he obtained by barter with the coal boats as they worked their way up or down the flight. A good-sized bucket-full for twenty Woodbines became established as the going rate. Fred became Jock's agent, taking orders, some of which were collected on passing and some of which were delivered to Long Buckby for collection by boats up the Oxford or the Warwick and Birmingham. Orders were coming in from London, from up the Paddington Arm and as far as Limehouse and the East End. In short, Jock was doing a roaring trade making a small fortune. Fred wasn't doing too badly either; his commission mounting up quite considerably.

Everything commanded a high price especially some of the ex-army 'souvenir' deals. The sales of consumables and luxury goods, watches and the like, whilst illicit, were less likely to attract attention but since such items were hard to come by, they too fetched very high prices from people who were all too willing to pay. On the shadier side of trade there were some genuine crooks developing an interest. East End villains had somehow got wind of the fact that firearms and other wartime 'equipment' was available. Not unduly concerned, in fact relieved if anything, Jock was happy to offload all the guns and weapons that he and Ken had accumulated. The armoury was the one line the business was carrying that otherwise might have been difficult to 'fence'. With the exception of just the one handgun, the Luger which had become his own personal pistol, and a quantity of ammunition, the whole arsenal was disposed of at premium rates and a quite staggeringly enormous profit. In return for the 'no questions asked' style of transactions with his 'friends' at Limehouse Docks, other goods from ships unloading cargoes from abroad and from the barges which plied the Pool of London were finding their way courtesy of retuning boats up the Grand Union and the Leicester Line for delivery to the *Emily Rose* at Foxton, with

Fred collecting the tolls, obviously. This way Jock was never short of merchandise.

With Easter and Whitsun over, Jock decided that the time had come to find a new pitch and keep his rendezvous with Helen. He and Fred spent one last evening together in the pub and relived some of their most lucrative and dishonourable dealings. Fred admitted that Jock's 'business' presence at Foxton had always been something of a worry to him and that he would not be sorry to see the back of it. With Jock gone Fred would sleep more easily. Even so he suspected that Jock would be back sooner or later.

The following morning bright and early Jock was about to fire up the Russell Newbury when a familiar sight caught his eye parked on the quay. A motorcycle. An Ariel 350.

'Bugger!' Jock exclaimed. A quick getaway was required here but of all mornings, whether it was the fault of Mr Russell or Mr Newbery, their engine just would not start.

'Yo' need t' get that looked at me ol' mate,' came the all too familiar voice.

'Och, Ron, ma friend.' Jock gave him a big smile. Then reaching to the waistband of his trousers he withdrew the Luger and shot the bus conductor in the centre of his forehead. Having never fired a shot in anger during the war he had now notched up three kills. Ron was the victim of an impulsive knee-jerk reaction just as the first two of Jock's victims had been. He scrambled on to the quay and dragged Ron's body into the hold of the *Emily Rose* before he was spotted by anyone. He then went looking for Fred.

'A pal ay mine wants me t' deliver a motorcycle tae Leicester. D'ye hev a plank I could borrow so's I can wheel it aboard?' With the Ariel safely stowed in the other end of the hold, Russell and Newbery both obliged. Jock cast off with the intention of completing his journey to Kilby Wharf where he had arranged to meet Helen all those months ago.

Chapter Eighteen

Having another dead body to dispose of was a complication Jock had not been anticipating. He had the Saddington Tunnel to navigate and several locks to work before he reached the trysting place. Jock's method of corpse disposal was tried and tested and so far had proved to be entirely satisfactory. From his present situation though the same means of getting rid of a corpse were hardly practical. Ideally he needed a van. He knew that even with the best will in the world he would not be able to strap Ron on the pillion of the Ariel for a trip to Upperton Road and the bridge over the goods yard. A plan B was desperately needed.

As *Emily Rose* approached bridge Number 72, Jock thought about mooring up and walking into Smeeton Westerby or Kibworth with the sole intention of 'borrowing' a van. He soon abandoned this idea as a non-starter. Whilst the addition of the theft of a vehicle to his charge sheet was fairly insignificant given the crimes he would already be indicted for the risk of being discovered was too great.

As he approached the tunnel there was a sudden change in the weather. What had been a fairly bright morning with warm sunny periods became cloudy and the chill in the air was such that Jock went below to get his jacket. There was something about this stretch of the waterway between the

Smeeton Aqueduct and the Saddington Tunnel that made him distinctly uneasy. The boat glided into the tunnel. It was pitch black. After the slightly ghostly experience of the Braunston and Husbands Bosworth tunnels he did have a touch of the jitters but the sensation here was weird, abnormal. Whatever it was, it gave Jock the creeps and he pushed the *Emily Rose* to full ahead in a panic to be through the tunnel as quickly as possible. As he emerged into the daylight, the weather was instantly restored to that typical of an early summer's day.

'That was the scariest 880 yards I've ever travelled,' he thought briefly as he took his jacket off. Then he thought no more about it.

Round the bend was Kibworth Top Lock. There was a boat already in the lock but it appeared to be coming towards him which was good news for Jock. Unless there was another boat a short distance ahead of him, the next three locks at least, Kibworth Number 19, Taylor's Number 20, and Pywell's Number 21 would all be made ready for him with the water at his level. And they were. He cleared these three locks as easily as an old boatman although he looked nothing like one. The Russell Newbery purred on and Jock didn't have a care, or so it seemed. It had turned into a lovely day and for all the world as he sat there on the stern rail, the tiller under his arm, it appeared that he had completely forgotten Ron's corpse just sixty-odd feet forward of him.

Another boat had just cleared Crane's Lock, Number 22. As they passed Jock recognised *The Mistress Martha* and the boatman who had bought six bottles of cognac a few weeks previous when he came through Foxton. They exchanged a bit of friendly banter.

There was not too far to go now. Jock took a look at his chart. Then it dawned on him that Helen might want to come aboard and check over the cargo. The last thing she would want to find would be the corpse of a dead bus conductor. The most undemanding and convenient means of 'lightening his load' now was to provide Ron with a watery grave. He drew into the bank just after bridge Number 77. On the left was an area of woodland. On the right he could hear a passing train. 'I wonder if that's a goods? It might be the 'boys' on the way to their final resting place' he thought to himself with a chuckle. 'Now then Ron, a watery grave or would yo' rather I plant yo' in the woods?' Jock was imitating Ron's dialect whilst mumbling through the choices to himself. He stepped ashore and made a warp fast to a tree. He wandered off into the spinney to give further reasoned consideration to his options. Talking out loud to himself, although addressing Ron, 'It'll nae be a grave in the woods," he concluded, and by way of justification for his decision, "I hiv'nae got a spade fur a start."

He climbed back aboard and into the hold. There was Ron's body. And there were the sacks containing the aggregate that Ron himself had swept up at the time they were loading the boat back in Hinckley. Jock found some rope with which he bound the necks of the two sacks. He tested their weight. 'Aye they are heavy right enough,' he thought. He tied one bag by binding the end of the rope around Ron's ankles, the other in similar fashion around his wrists. He checked Ron's pockets to remove any means of identification he may have been carrying and whilst he was at it he relieved Ron of the cash and coupons he had. Jock was ready and so was Ron. He restarted the engine, pulled in his warp and headed into midstream. Just ahead now was the village of Newton Harcourt. This local area was a little more like familiar territory. Just beyond Newton was Great Glen. He'd driven the bus route there a few times. He entered the Newton Top Lock, Number 23.

'Here?' he asked himself. 'Nae!'

Clearing Number 23, it was only a short stretch to Number 22, Spinney Lock.

'Here?' He noticed a couple of people walking over bridge Number 81. 'Nae!'

Down then to Number 25, the Top Half Mile Lock. As he guided the boat through the gates he took a good look around. The towpath was on the right, the north side of the canal, on the left, some woodland.

'Here'll dae!' Having secured the boat to the bollards and closed the gates. Jock went into the hold and folded the cover back sufficiently to heave the body on to the gunnel then one by one drop the sacks of aggregate over the side dragging the body with them. There was barely a splash. A few air bubbles broke the surface after which the uninviting black water returned to its state of stillness and nothing.

Jock replaced the tarpaulin cover over the hold, and then raised the paddles on the top gates. The lock emptied and as the levels equalised Jock eased the boat clear but only by a few feet. He nudged into the bank, stepped ashore taking a warp with him and wrapped it around the handrail on the lock steps. He closed the gates and took a long hard look into the murky depths, or were they now shallows where he'd dropped the body. Although the water level was much lower there was no sign of a body or of the weighted sacks. He opened the paddles of the lower gate and refilled the lock before getting back aboard and shoving off. There was only a very short distance to run now with four more locks. He was looking forward to meeting Helen and having a few pints in the Navigation Inn at Kilby Wharf.

As *Emily Rose* tied up at Kilby Wharf Helen and two others approached.

'Hello again Jock. This is Ernie, Frank's brother, his daughter, Kate, and, indicating the baby which Kate was carrying, 'my son, Ken's son, Ben.'

Chapter Nineteen

After the niceties of the introductions, Ernie drove Kate with Ben in her arms back to the farm at Kilby. Jock and Helen waved goodbye and went into the Navigation Inn. Helen was anxious to know all about Jock's adventures and over several drinks lasting as many hours Jock related every detail, apart from one or two. Helen was most interested to hear how the initial sales had come about so quickly with the best part of £300-worth of goods being sold in the first two days. Jock implied that it might have been something to do with his charm and persuasive nature! Helen's relief was quite visibly apparent when Jock told her that the weapons, their accessories and ammunition had all been sold. However she had reservations about the buyers and their intentions with the merchandise they had acquired. The reputation and influence of East End gangsters had long extended as far as the Midlands. Jock assured her that there was no way the guns could be traced back to them. Altogether, Helen was delighted in the way in which everything had developed since their meeting in the Cross Keys those several months ago. They now had, thanks to Jock, a successful and profitable enterprise dealing with goods of dubious provenance. Helen excused herself to visit the toilet and as she rose from the table she leaned over and kissed Jock on the cheek.

Upon her return, Jock had ordered more drinks and wanted to know the status of Helen's relationship with Ken. He knew that after their fight Ken had disappeared but little else. Helen spoke of Albert's speculative letter and how it had in fact reached the intended recipient. With the slightest tinge of sadness in her voice she let Jock know that as far as she was concerned her marriage was over. Ken knew he had a son. Albert had told him. So why, and she told her story with tears in her eyes, had Ken made no effort to make contact with her or offer any support, financial or otherwise. The question was rhetorical. What Helen found quite bizarre was the fact that he had made no enquiry at all about the turnover of what had become her business with Jock particularly since he had been so heavily involved in the establishment of the enterprise and the acquisition of the stock.

They had much to discuss. Helen told Jock all about Frank and how he had made the accommodation arrangements with Ernie. She told him all about Ben's birth and the family gatherings they had enjoyed. Jock seemed to be very impressed. He wanted to know whether there had been any unwanted attention of any description; police or others asking awkward questions? He casually asked after the people who had lived upstairs. Helen really didn't know. She hadn't seen them 'for ages'. Jock smiled but his smile disappeared when she mentioned that Frank had been arrested for handling stolen property.

Altogether they had spent a pleasant evening together and Jock's disappointment could not be mistaken when Helen announced that Ernie was coming to collect her. He had been harbouring high hopes for some rather intimate female company aboard the *Emily Rose*. Still he was encouraged by her announcement that the marriage was over.

Ernie arrived at closing time with just enough time for a

swift half. With Ernie waiting in the car Helen suggested that provided she could get Kate to look after Ben she would come to inspect the boat and its contents the following day. She went to great lengths to impress upon Jock that Ernie and Kate should be kept totally in the dark and in complete ignorance of what the two of them were about.

Helen returned to the wharf the next day. This time, she been driven there by Frank. Jock stepped off the boat.

'Aye, well, it's grand t' see ye both!' he said, quite genuinely.

'Grand, is it? We'll hev' t' see about that.' Frank replied.

'Now then, you two,' Helen scolded. 'Jock, have you got the kettle on?'

The three of them climbed aboard and went into the cramped but cosy boatman's cabin and drank the tea that Jock had made. Frank made his excuses, went ashore and filled his pipe.

Jock gave Helen a tour of the hold pointing out which of the stores were which and from where and which had been recently purchased, bartered for, borrowed, or otherwise acquired. Helen enquired about the Ariel.

'Doesn't that belong to your friend, the chap you were on the buses with?'

Jock hedged his response. 'It wis his, a'reet. He's got a van the noo and has lent me the bike should I need tae goo anywhere."

Whilst Helen carried out her inspection Frank paced up and down the quay puffing away at his pipe. He really wasn't interested in this illicit business Helen had got herself involved with especially after his own brush with the law. He was concerned about Helen's welfare though and highly suspicious of Jock and his motives.

After Helen had inspected the book that Jock had kept albeit partially and most of which was a work of fiction, she expressed her satisfaction in return for which Jock handed her a substantial package wrapped in a double page from the *Daily Herald*.

'Dinnae look the noo, wait 'til ye get hame. I've taken some t' cover expenses and this is your share ay the profits so far.'

With an agreement that Jock would stay at the wharf for the next few days during which she would come to visit again, Helen made to depart but not before Frank had issued a cautionary word in Jock's ear, delivered with menace.

'Yo' do right by my Helen or yo'll live to regret it.'

When Helen was back at her cottage with Ben tucked up and fast asleep, she remembered the Daily Herald package and retrieved it from her handbag. She tore the paper open to reveal a thick bundle of banknotes; mainly £5 notes, but with £1 and ten-shilling notes too. Never had Helen seen so much money. She counted and recounted. Three-thousand-six-hundred-and forty-two pounds, ten shillings.

Chapter Twenty

Helen was both astonished and bewildered. What would she do with such fortune? Her mind began to race excitedly at the prospect of so many possibilities. But first where should she put it. She didn't have a bank account. She fetched her biscuit tin from the kitchen, ate the last two remaining biscuits (Kate baked delicious biscuits) and squeezed the money into the tin. She then hid the tin under her winter cardigan in the wardrobe.

Not wishing to impose unreasonably on Kate yet again Helen got a lift to Albert and Mabel's house taking Ben with her. Ernie stopped the car for her to call in the village shop to buy Mabel a box of chocolates. Albert and Mabel were of course absolutely delighted to see Ben and only too pleased to look after him for a few hours while Helen 'did a few errands'. In fact there were only two 'errands'. Living in the middle of nowhere Helen needed the ability to get about independently. She wanted to see Frank with a view to getting some driving lessons. She'd learnt to drive the tractor during the war and felt she could manage a motor-car without too much difficulty. She could of course now afford to buy herself one.

She also needed to see Jock again; to thank him for the money and, believing him to be interested in her, offer a little encouragement as a means to the business relationship continuing. That way would ensure a regular income after that incredible first instalment for the foreseeable future.

Helen had already prepared Ben's 'Cow & Gate' bottle. It would just have stand in some hot water for a while to warm it up. There was also a box of Farley's Rusks and a couple of clean Terry Towel nappies in the 'baby bag'. She left in a hurry saying she'd be back in two or three hours.

Frank was tinkering with the tractor again when she arrived in his yard. Explaining the reason for her visit in addition to the social call obviously Frank was flattered to have been asked. He'd pick her up this evening and she could have her first lesson straight away.

'Could I start right now, I mean are you too busy? It's ok, Ben's with his Grannie. I need to see Jock. It's very important. I'll only need to be a little while. I can get some petrol coupons.' With Helen's flurry of questions and the pitch of her excitement, anyone would have imagined she was a little girl again. How could Frank possibly resist?

'Gi' me a minute to get cleaned up a bit, and slow down,' he laughed.

After a couple of false starts Helen had got the measure of the clutch, and ably drove the car perfectly well to Kilby Wharf although she needed to gain a little more road-sense. She all but ran onto the *Emily Rose* where Jock sat on the stern rail. Frank had no wish to see Jock so he decided to go for a stroll along the towpath with his pipe.

Helen threw her arms around Jock almost precipitating him into the canal. She gave him a huge hug and kissed him in a manner which was not totally devoid of passion.

'Dinnae stop there lassie,' urged Jock, so she didn't.

They went into the cabin and sat on the sofa which doubled as the bed. After five minutes Helen decided that things were getting a little too heated and besides which that was enough encouragement, for now at least.

Being the man of the world that he considered himself to be, knowing a thing or two about the workings of the female mind, or so he thought, Jock recognised that this most enjoyable exposition of emotion he had just been on the receiving end of was Helen's way of thanking him for the cash. If so, was this not a basis for establishing a relationship which would deliver more?

'Wul ye look the noo, Helen, I ken it's short notice an' stuff, but ahm goin' back doon to Foxton in a couple ay days. It'd be grand if ye'd...'

'I'd love to.' Helen had accepted the invitation before Jock had completed its issue.

Had she thought through the implications? No. Had she given consideration to what she would do with Ben? No. Had she thought about what she would say to Frank, to Ernie or Kate, to Albert and Mabel? No. No. No. It was all wrong.

The smell of smouldering St Bruno drifting into *Emily Rose*'s cabin could only mean one thing. Helen retied her hair back, straightened her dress and blowing Jock a kiss she left the boat. Not a lot was said on the drive back. Helen was in the driving seat and proving herself to be perfectly competent. Frank sat next to her, the volume of his body language shouting and screaming disapproval of what he suspected had come to pass in the last hour. When they arrived to pick up Ben, Helen turned to Frank and gave him a look, totally free from guilt inviting him to say something. How long had he been standing by the boat? Had he overheard anything of the conversation? Helen wondered. Eventually Frank did speak.

'Go on an' fetch the boy an' I'll drive you both home.' The manner in which he spoke was emphatically disapproving. Helen got out of the car and minutes later returned with Ben. When they were back at Helen's cottage at Kilby, it occurred to Frank that they were only a short walk from the wharf where the *Emily Rose* was moored. He gave Helen the look that he might have given to a fallen angel.

'I bloody well hope you know what you're a-doin' of my girl. I sincerely do.' And with this parting comment he drove off.

Helen went into her cottage, fed, bathed and dressed Ben and laid him down to sleep. She made herself some tea and began to weep as she considered and reconsidered what she was about to do. Frank was probably her greatest friend and his attitude coupled with the few words that he had spoken had given Helen real cause to doubt herself; her personal motives. Was her self-interest now driven by this real potential for wealth beyond her wildest dreams. She was in a real quandary.

She didn't sleep at all well that night, partly because Ben was awake and crying for most of it and partly because she was wrestling with her conscience. Ben's crying wasn't helping. Had Helen's maternal instincts evaporated? Did she really relish the prospect of being a single mother and raising a child on her own? If she went off with Jock, how would her family view her degeneracy, the scandal? What would her friends make of her fall from grace? She wasn't a bad person – or maybe she was just for having these thoughts. There again would she be suited to an itinerant existence and on the periphery of a life of crime if not slap bang at the epicentre? These and many more ethical intellectual processes were subjected to Helen's reasoning power. However, her rationality finally gave way to the mental image of piles of cash.

Yes she decided, to hell with it all. She could abandon everything and everyone and sail off with Jock into the unknown. Helen felt she could get to like him and even share his bed despite her previous and quite determined statement that she had no intention of becoming a boat-man's floozy. Reparation would be in the form of the piles of cash that now seemed to be clouding all her rational thought and consideration.

When it came to deciding what should happen to Ben, Helen didn't have too many alternatives. It would not be practical to take him with her. She was aware that boat people lived on board and brought up families in the very confined spaces that were available on a working narrow-boat. But that was perhaps because they couldn't afford to live ashore. She could leave him with Kate and visit every time the *Emily Rose* passed through Kilby. But Helen was very fond of Kate. She was a young woman for whom it wouldn't be long before she found a man she would want to settle down with. How many men would be willing to take on another's stepchild? No, there was only one option. It would have to be the grandparents. Helen would go and discuss the situation with them at the earliest opportunity.

The next day, Helen asked Kate to babysit whilst she walked to Kilby Wharf to see Jock.

He was of course more than delighted to see her. The reason for her visit was to beg the favour of a ride into Hinckley to see Albert and Mabel. She felt that asking Ernie for a lift wasn't really on. She didn't want to have to tell him lies about the purpose of her visit, and Ernie being the sociable sort, he would want to come in and have tea, and chat. Jock rigged the gangplank and wheeled the Ariel onto the quayside. Helen had never ridden on a motorcycle before and this in itself was exciting. Upon arrival at Albert and Mabel's house, she instructed Jock to make himself scarce. She would meet him in an hour at the Cross Keys.

Helen really didn't know how to broach the subject. Albert and Mabel were of course pleased to see her as always and made the customary enquiries after the welfare of their grandson. Helen responded with evasive small talk. She made several hesitant beginnings but in the end couldn't actually bring herself to say what she wanted to say. The more she tried, the more apparent it became to Albert and Mabel that all was not as it ought to be. Finally, Helen chose to lie.

'Rosemary, my sister, has the opportunity to go to the seaside at Skegness for the weekend with some the old land-army girls and she's asked me to go with her. I'd really like to go but the problem is…' Before she could actually explain what the problem was in this fictional scenario, Mabel had intervened.

'Of course my dear we'd love to look after Ben for a few days wouldn't we Albert?' Albert's response took the form of a brief smile which slowly transfigured into a look of horror.

So that was settled and Ben's welfare was assured for a few days at least. Although it would be a rift to be separated from her son, Helen had no intention of them being reunited for the foreseeable future if at all. She had every confidence of him being well looked after and brought up nicely. To assuage her maternal neglect and dishonesty, she would send money for Ben's upkeep, clothes and the like. Such an act of charitable responsibility, as she convinced herself, would ease her guilt.

On the Friday of that week Ben was delivered with all his baby paraphernalia including the 'Silver Cross' to Albert and Mabel's house. Helen handed her son over to Mabel having given him a final kiss and cuddle. Not that she knew it then, but they would not see each other for some considerable time. In the interests of consistency Helen used the same 'land-army reunion at Skegness' excuse with Kate and Ernie. Having packed a bag with her essentials not forgetting the biscuit tin, of course, Helen bade farewell to the couple who had been so hospitable, kind and caring; the couple who had come to her rescue when she was desperate. She didn't know when, or even if she might ever see them again.

She walked off down the lane from the farmhouse. Kate and Ernie stood and waved. They didn't notice her mount the pillion of a motorcycle.

Chapter Twenty-One

On Saturday morning, Jock was up early. He made Helen a cup of tea and passed it to her in bed.

'I could get used to this.'

'Aye, ahm hoping ye wull."

They had spent the previous evening sitting and chatting in the cabin of the *Emily Rose*. Helen didn't want to be seen by anyone who might recognise her when she was supposed to be on her way to Skegness. So the pub was given a miss. Once it was dark they had risked being out on the small open deck at the helmsman's position and had sat on the stern rails looking at the moonlight reflected on the limpid surface of the canal. When it came to bedtime, Jock, ever the gentleman had allowed Helen the privacy of changing into her nightdress and getting into bed before he joined her. Helen had been unsure, but Jock again proved he knew how to behave like a gentleman. It had been a comfortable if cosy night in the bijou cabin. Helen, despite herself, had snuggled up to Jock and enjoyed the sensation of lying next to a man again; a man who treated her like a lady.

Early next morning Helen dressed while Jock put the frying pan on the stove.

'Bacon!' exclaimed Helen already salivating. 'Where did you get the coupons from?'

'Och, dinnae be so sully!'

After breakfast, the Russell Newbery had the *Emily Rose* on her way south back to Foxton. They soon approached bridge Number 84 which all but combined with lock Number 29, the so-called 'Bumblebee' lock. Helen was fascinated. Looking under the bridge she could just see the lock-gates, firmly closed.

'How do we get in?' It was all clearly a mystery to Helen. Jock loosely secured the boat in the 'waiting' area whilst he explained the principles behind the workings of a lock. Then he led Helen ashore and whilst giving a more detailed account of what he was up to he raised the paddles in the upper gates. Helen stared in awe as the water rushed through and the levels on both sides of the gates equalised, allowing them to be opened.

'Aye now, you stay there an' I'll bring the boat in. When she's in, you close the gates behind us,' instructed Jock. And, with the boat in the lock, he shouted the next set of instructions up to Helen on the lockside.

'Drop the paddles in the upper gates, tak' care noo, mind yer fingers. Right, noo open the paddles in the lower gates.'

Helen wasn't stupid, and as an ex-land-army girl, she was fairly strong, and understood what had to be done. She completed the locking through the Bumblebee without any further instructions being required.

'Well now, seems you're a natural,' complimented Jock. 'We've got several more locks tae get through so if ye dinnae mind, take the windlass, walk tae the next, and make the lock ready.'

Helen did as Jock had bidden and walked off at a slightly quicker pace than the boat. By the time *Emily Rose* had arrived at Number 28, Tythorn Lock, the gates were open and the lock ready. The next two, Turnover Lock Number 27 and Number 26 the Bottom Half-Mile Lock, were also ready when the boat reached them. Just before Helen strode off to Number 25, Jock called her to get on board. He'd spotted a boat heading towards them from Number 25, so no preparation would be required. Jock also need to check on the integrity of Number 25's secret. They waved to the boatman and his wife on the *Sheldrake* as they passed and fifty yards ahead of the Top Half-Mile Jock took the engine out of gear and glided sufficiently slowly to allow him to make his way forward on the boat so that he could search the water in the lock whilst at its lower level. The boat very gently nudged the gates and came to a halt. Helen was curious as to what he was up to.

'Is there something I should know about here?'

'Och nae, I dropped summat in yon lock, last time through. I wis wonderin' whether I could see it. That's all.' Jock was being truthful for once!

'What did you drop?'

'Nothin' for ye tae worry aboot. C'mon let's get crackin'.' With that, the locking through Number 25 was completed and the *Emily Rose* continued her journey towards Foxton. With *Sheldrake* on its way north, the locks were all prepared for *Emily Rose* heading south. After Numbers 24 and 23, there was time to put the kettle on and have another cup of tea. The morning was pleasantly warm and Helen sat on the stern rail opposite Jock standing with the tiller under his arm. From Cranes up to Kibworth Top Lock Number 18, everything was perfect. Helen had not been as content as she was at this time since her honeymoon in the Peak District. She loved the countryside and the opportunity to see it at a leisurely pace from a narrowboat on a canal, following natural contours on the fields was a brand-new experience for her. Since leaving all her previous existence behind, this, she thought, is as good as it gets.

As they approached Ross Bridge, Number 74, Jock's

demeanour changed. He gave up on the commentary he'd been providing and became quite agitated. He was fidgeting and casting anxious glances all around as if expecting some misfortune or calamity.

'Jock, whatever's wrong?' Helen was genuinely concerned.

'I dinnae ken whit it is aboot it, but yon tunnel up ahead, the Saddington Tunnel just gis me the creeps.' He recalled the sensations he had previously experienced with this tunnel but Helen made little of what she rather regarded as an irrationality. With a disregard for her ridiculing what he was feeling, Jock declared, 'Ye can mock but ye'll see whit I mean in a minute.' They entered the tunnel. It was pitch black. Helen shivered. There was definitely something ethereal, abstract, non-existent yet tangible. Whatever it was, it was inexplicable. As before, Jock rammed the throttle forward and *Emily Rose* responded. They emerged from the tunnel and Helen looked back at what now appeared to be nothing more or less than a very uninviting black hole.

'Did ye nae feel it?" Jock asked

'No, not a thing. You're getting paranoid!' scoffed Helen with a laugh.

Jock was visibly relieved and Helen thought maybe she had been unkind in making light of his apprehension in the way she had.

'I'm sorry Jock. I didn't mean to make fun of you, but really, it's only a tunnel after all.'

'Aye, maybe you're right. Jes' masel bein' stupid.'

Nothing more was mentioned about the Saddington experience and an hour later they were tied up outside the Foxton Locks Inn.

Chapter Twenty-Two

It was Sunday night. Mabel was listening to the wireless. Felton Rapley, the celebrity organist was broadcasting from the organ at the Dominion Theatre. Albert was dozing in his chair. The programme came to an end. It was 11 pm.

'Would you like some cocoa, dear?' Mabel asked.

'Is Helen still not back? I hope nothing's happened.'

The grandparents had enjoyed their weekend looking after Ben. He'd not been any trouble at all. In fact they'd proudly walked him around the town in his 'Silver Cross' and many people had stopped them and remarked upon 'such a bonny baby', not that he was still a baby. He was growing up fast. But now they were looking forward to handing him back to his mother and getting back to their own routine as distinct from adjusting to Ben's. His baby bag was all packed and ready to go but as Mabel observed,

'It's very late, and it doesn't seem right that we'll have to wake him up. Better he stays until the morning.' Albert had to agree. They drank their cocoa and went to bed.

As babies are wont to do Ben was awake early gurgling away with the dawn chorus. Mabel dragged herself out of bed and gave him a rusk to be going with whilst she got dressed. At breakfast the grandparents were beginning to get concerned about the non-arrival of their daughter-in-law.

'Well, there's not a great deal we can do is there? May be the bus broke down?' Mabel offered.

Monday became Tuesday. Wednesday ran into Thursday. Still no Helen nor any word from her. Albert had already had to go to the chemist for some more milk powder and rusks. Mabel had washed the nappies several times now as well.

'I'll go to Rosemary's house. Maybe what's his name, Neville, might have some news.'

Albert was surprised when Rosemary opened the door. His surprise was compounded when she informed him that she knew nothing of any land-army reunion or trips to Skegness. On his way home he stopped at the police station. PC Almey was on duty.

'Hello Albert, what brings you here?'

'I need to report a missing person.'

Albert went on to describe the situation as he understood it to be; his concern that something untoward had befallen Helen, not to mention the fact that he was becoming weary of babysitting even though the baby in question was his grandson. PC Almey had made notes and promised he would speak to his sergeant and initiate a search. They would start by telephoning the Lincolnshire Constabulary and get them to make enquiries in Skegness. Helpfully the constable also suggested that he would go and see if Frank might have any ideas.

After another couple days during which there had been no developments in establishing Helen's whereabouts or recent movements, Frank's Austin drew up outside Albert's house.

More in hope than expectation Albert invited Frank in. Mabel made tea and they sat in the parlour.

'I 'aven't told Gordon Almey. I thought yo' should know first.'

'Know what?'

'I reckon our Helen's gone off the rails. She's bin seein' that Scotsman, Jock – he who were in the army wi' your Ken. I reckon she might 'ave gone off wi' 'im somewhere.'

'She'd never do that, what and leave Ben here with us? No, she'd never do that!' Mabel was quite adamant. Frank admitted that he'd taken her to Kilby Wharf where she'd met with Jock. But he emphasised that he also brought her back.

'Does Ernie not have any idea?'

'No, I've bin to Ernie's and she'd told 'im an' Kate about some land-army knees-up that she were a-goin' to at the seaside somewhere. We've looked in her cottage an' there's no clues there. Could she have gone after Ken?'

'It's only us who have got any idea where Ken is. And as far as I can make out, Ken doesn't want anyone else to know.'

Just as Frank was about leave, Gordon Almey arrived on his bike.

'We've just had word from Skegness police station that nobody there knows anything about a land-army reunion. There've been no reports of anything that would lead us believe that Helen's been involved in an accident or any-thing like that. She just seems to have disappeared. If there's nothing else you can tell me we'll just have to wait and see if she turns up or we get any leads.' And then, quite inad-vertently and without realising it, Gordon Almey identified the crux of the matter.

'Maybe she doesn't want to be found.' They sat in silent disbelief.

Gordon asked for a photograph that could be circulated. Mabel produce one taken at Helen and Ken's wedding. She took a long look at it as she handed it over. She then picked Ben up from the rug where he'd been lying, held him close to her and began to cry.

Gordon and Frank left the distressed grandparents.

'What are we to do then? What about this poor little mite?' Mabel continued to weep.

'The first thing we need to do is get our Ken back here. He's the father and should have a say in what happens to his son.'

Albert's suggestion seemed eminently sensible to Mabel and she cheered up a little.

'I'll see if I can get him on the telephone. If not I'll have to write I suppose. In the meantime, it'll have to be me and you who takes care of the boy.'

Later that day, armed with a pocketful of loose change, Albert walked to the nearest telephone kiosk two streets away. He called the operator and pessimistically asked if she could put him through to Fort George. She couldn't find the listing. Ken's letter had been very brief and he hadn't provided an address or telephone number. Albert was therefore obliged to try and make contact again though Fort George and the only way would be to write.

That evening he spent several hours composing a letter and he made many attempts before he was satisfied with what he had committed to paper. The letter was posted the next day.

Chapter Twenty-Three

It was October, almost three months since Albert had written to his son; a letter to which there had been no response. Ben was now sitting up unaided, and eating 'proper' baby food. It had been many years since their children had been Ben's age and Albert and Mabel's parenting skills had long been forgotten. Even so they were doing a reasonable job or so they felt. At least Ben's birth had now been registered and Ben had been checked over at the health clinic. Toilet training would be on the agenda next. Albert was really looking forwards to this!

There was a knock at the door.

'Who can that possibly be?' asked Mabel, her arms up the elbows in a bucket of nappies.

'Happen it's Helen.' Albert opened the door and immediately took two paces backwards.

'Ken, my son and with a beard! Hey Mabel, you'll never guess who's turned up.'

'Watcha dad. Hello mam,' he shouted through the kitchen. Mabel came bustling through to the hallway drying her hands on her apron. She grasped him by the shoulders.

'Here, let's have a look at you.'

'Let the lad in then mother,' ordered Albert.

They went into the living room. Ben was sitting on a rug on the floor chewing on a teething ring.

' Who's this then?' enquired Ken.

'Ben, meet your dad,' Albert said. Ken bent down and gathered his son up into his arms.

'It would have been nice if you could have let us know you were coming' said Albert disappointedly.

'I did. Didn't you get my letter?'

'We got a letter months and months ago when you said you'd try and get some leave.'

'There you are then. I did let you know!' Ken was sitting now bouncing Ben on his knee. Ben was giggling and enjoying it as much as Ken was.

'Where's Helen?' asked Ken.

'That's what we'd like to know,' replied his dad

'What do you mean?' Ken was looking quizzically at his father then at his mother.

'I explained everything in my letter' said Albert. It was only then they all suddenly realised that Albert's second letter had not been received.

The rest of the day was spent in going over every detail of Helen's disappearance. Ken said nothing of his guilty conscience; that the reason she had disappeared was more than likely his fault. He said nothing about the domestic abuse he had subjected her to. He said nothing of his black marketeering or the breakdown of his relationship with Jock. He said nothing of his fight with Jock or the murder of the two tenants with whom he and Helen had shared a house. He said nothing of his near mental breakdown and the desperate need he felt to get away. Maybe all of this was best left unsaid. Ben had fallen asleep on Ken's knee. Mabel took him up in her arms,

'I'll put him down for the night,' she whispered.

Albert retrieved the bottle of scotch Ken had presented

him with when he came home from the war. It had so far been unopened, but now seemed like good time.

'I am so truly sorry dad for the way things have all turned out. I'm surprised that Helen walked out on the baby though. I know I didn't treat her as well as I should have done. I didn't share her enthusiasm for becoming a parent. I'd got so much more on my mind at the time. If I could have that time back I do it all differently.' Albert sat and listened. There was some sympathy and understanding in his expression but he wanted to know more. He needed to know more.

'Are you in trouble lad? Have you got on the wrong side of the law?' Albert knew how to open Ken up and it was with humility and respect that Ken answered.

'I was dad,' Ken admitted. 'It's why I ran away. I'm not going to give you all the details, but I will tell you this. I was involved with a bloke in the army, doing a bit of wheeling and dealing. I think you suspected this. It all got out of hand when we got home and if the police had got involved I'd be in prison now as an accomplice or worse. That's all in the past now – well I hope it is. I want to wipe the slate clean and make a fresh start and when I'm sure that the past has all blown over I'm going to come back and start again and look after my son. I can raise him on my own if need be. We'll be OK.'

'So what are your plans? What are going do?'

'I've got to go back to Scotland for a while. I can't just go AWOL and I don't want a dishonourable discharge on my record. I'm sure you understand that better than most. If you and mam don't mind another few months of looking after Ben I'll find us a house and we'll be a proper family.' The apparent sincerity of Ken's speech had moved his dad.

'I'll talk to your mother. It'll all depend on her. She'll have most of the responsibility. If it's OK with her, it's OK with me.'

Ken went upstairs to the room where Ben was now fast asleep and for the first time a father kissed his son. He stood gazing into the cot for quite a while.

During the next two weeks whilst he was on leave Ken got to know his son. Fed him, bathed him in the sink, dressed him, changed him, wiped his backside as and when required and did all of those things that would normally be expected of a mother. But not without guidance, instruction and supervision from his own mother! He pushed Ben into the town and they visited the town hall and the council office to get their names put on the waiting list for a council house or a prefab. He also took the opportunity to check on his nest-egg with George in Great Glen, which had been the main point of his trip south.

With a promise to keep in touch regularly Ken went back to the Cultybraggan Camp and Albert and Mabel became the formal guardians of their grandson until such time as Ken left the army for good and came home.

It all seemed to be an acceptable solution under the circumstances.

Chapter Twenty-Four

Albert and Mabel were well into their sixties. Looking after a baby of less than a year old, fulltime, was the last thing they might have imagined themselves doing. There were certain ameliorating features to the situation though. In truth they both enjoyed having Ben in the house. Had there not been moderating factors to this predicament the imposition would have been intolerable. Albert and Mabel were both very aware that the formative years of a child's life and the manner in which the child was brought up impacted on the rest of the child's life. In so many ways those first few years determined the sort of person the child would become. At Ben's age stability and routine were the key according to Albert. When Ken was small, as first-time parents they had made mistakes. Those mistakes proved to be lessons to be learned and they had not been repeated with Peter or Jane, Ken's siblings. Albert was far from convinced that Helen and Ken would not have made mistakes and anyway, with Ken away in the army and Helen goodness knows where, it was down to Mabel and himself to bring up this child; to watch him grow, develop and become an individual of whom they could be proud. Besides, what were the alternatives? An orphanage? Having him fostered or adopted by unknowns? Unlikely? Not likely!

Albert himself had been in the army from a boy of fourteen. He'd known discipline and self-control. He'd been taught respect and obedience. Ben would be taught the same lessons but not by the 'carrot and the stick' method that Albert had endured. No, he would deploy the 'iron fist in the velvet glove'. Somehow he just knew that Ken would default on his promises. It would be years rather than months before Ken came home, he felt certain.

And thus it was that Ben was raised by his grandparents. They watched him learn to crawl. The potty training that Albert had so dreaded had not been a major issue at all. Frank, Ernie and Kate were invited for Ben's first Christmas and he delighted everyone by taking his first few faltering steps. In general he was a good baby; sleeping through the night and creating a minimum of inconvenience or unreasonable demands.

On his first birthday a card arrived, simply signed 'Mummy'. The postmark on the envelope was undiscernible. Inside the card was a money order to the value of £100. Albert opened a bank account in Ben's name.

As the weather improved the three of them would go to the Cross Keys and sit in the garden watching the village cricket on the recreation ground. Albert would insist on pushing Ben in the new pushchair he had bought out the 'Miscellaneous Sales' column of the local newspaper. The cost of the pushchair was more than met by the proceeds of the sale through the same column of the 'Silver Cross' pram the following week. Wherever they went Ben attracted a lot of attention; such a good-looking boy that he was. His grandparents were so very proud of him.

On his second birthday a card arrived, simply signed 'Mummy'. The postmark on the envelope was undiscernible. Inside the card was a money order to the value of £100. Albert paid the order into Ben's bank account.

Neither Albert nor Mabel were surprised that two

Christmases and two birthdays had passed and there had not been a single word from Ken. The greetings from 'Mummy' not to mention the generous monetary birthday contributions were an enormous surprise however. They both wondered how Helen was making her money but preferred not to give it too much thought.

Three more Christmases and three more birthdays. Nothing from his dad. Albert's suspicions had been proven. Ken may not have been forgotten but he was never mentioned. 'Mummy' on the other hand never forgot. Each birthday delivered a £100 money order.

Home life was fine. Ben's was a stable and routine existence. There were occasional new adventures; a visit to Frank's farm at lambing time went down very well indeed. He especially enjoyed riding his tricycle, a gift from 'uncle' Ernie and 'aunty' Kate. He was always around in the garden helping his grandad. Albert was now keeping chickens and feeding them and collecting the eggs was a daily highlight. Then it was time for school. Ben was enrolled in St Catherine's Church School for Infants.

On the day he came home from school on the sixth birthday Albert blindfolded Ben and lead him into the spare room, sat him on a stool and instructed him to reach forward with his arms. The sudden sounds startled him and he pulled the blindfold down – a piano.

The whoops of delight were a joy to behold.

'You're going to learn to play the piano,' said Albert. There was no question along the lines of 'would you like to?'. Oh no. Ben was to become a pianist and that was that.

'I'm a bit rusty, but I'm sure I can get you started,' said Albert with every confidence. Thus another bond between Ben and his grandad was established.

It was during the summer holidays when the stability faltered and routine was abandoned.

Ben was collecting eggs from the hen-house,

'Ben,' his grandad called down the garden. 'There's someone here you should meet.'

Ben took the eggs to the kitchen and went into the living room. His grandmother was in tears. His grandad was looking stern. Who was the other man? Ben wondered.

'Ben, meet you father.'

Ben burst into tears and went running upstairs to his bedroom.

It had happened. The day that Albert thought would never happen, and he was furious.

'Almost seven bloody years without a blasted word. Not a card or a letter and you think you can just come barging in here and upset everything!' Albert was extremely angry. Ben could hear the shouting from his room. He'd never heard his grandad raise his voice before. The argument continued for several minutes during which Albert's rage was maintained at boiling point. Even so, Ken's counterarguments and excuses kept coming. The atmosphere in the living room was hostile.

From Ben's perspective and his limited understanding of what the quarrelling was all about, this man; a man that Ben didn't know was his father but according to him Ben should be living with him and not with his grandfather. From what he could make out Ben was now expected to leave his grandparents' house and move in with this man that he didn't know. This was all very distressing but Ben couldn't see his grandad so upset; nor his grandma. Ben could hear she was still crying in the kitchen. He crept downstairs and for all that he was not yet seven years old he knew that he, Ben, was at the centre of all this unpleasantness. It wasn't right that there should be all this bickering and tension. Everyone in the house was part of the same family. He went into the kitchen and tried to console his grandma. He took her hand and lead her into the living room. Instantly, just by his very presence in the room the friction between his father and grandfather dissipated.

It was his grandfather who spoke first.

'Ben, I know this will be difficult for you and hard to understand but you have to move to live with your dad. You won't be moving far and you'll come to us every day after school for your tea and to do your piano practice.'

Ken stood silently with his eyes cast downwards. Mabel stood silently still holding Ben's hand. Ben looked quizzically at the man who was his dad.

'Will I have a mam as well?' It was Mabel who replied,

'Yes, you already have a mam but she lives somewhere else. It'll just be you and your dad for a while. You'll soon get to know each other.'

To Ben's way of thinking there seemed to be little or no point in contesting this arrangement or of making a fuss. Tantrums were not part of his psyche.

'Shall I go and get my things then?'

'Oh no you're not moving just yet. It'll be a few days because your dad has got to sort out a new house for you both. Now, go and see to the chickens while me and your dad discuss some of the details.'

Ken and Albert sat down and in a much calmer and almost submissive way Albert acknowledged that Ken, his son, as the boy's biological father, should be the responsible parent. But he also issued a cautionary warning.

'I'm giving in to you because I believe it's right that a child should live with its parents, or parent in your case. But I need you to promise me faithfully that you'll look after him properly and not go running away again. But if you don't turn up next week or in any way you break your promise to me….' Albert hesitated before pronouncing 'that's it!'

The veracious finality of the last two words was

unequivocal and for the avoidance of any doubt; not there could have been any.

'You mess up again, and even though I am your father, I will go to court and apply for legal custody of Ben and you will no longer be my son!'

'Ok dad, I'll do my best. I promise.'

'That all I ask son, that's all I've ever asked."

Chapter Twenty-Five

The dressing down that Ken had received from his father was more severe than any he had ever received from a superior officer in the army. He had left the house that day in a state of total demoralisation. It had been his perdition. The force of his father's temper coupled with his mother's distress had finally made him understand that he could not continue to behave as he had since coming home from the war. He had a responsibility which he now needed to take seriously. But would he?

He went directly to the Town Hall and the housing department. Yes, he was registered as a single parent and his name had risen to the top of the waiting list but when he didn't respond to the letters that the council had sent to him he was struck off. Not unreasonably the council had assumed he'd found somewhere else to live.

The gods must have been smiling on Ken that day in the council offices however. The council official accepted the excuse that Ken had offered, about him being unable to leave the army and the camp in Scotland. But the officer explained, as luck would have it, there was a two-bedroomed semidetached house on the new Brookside Estate which would be available at the beginning of the following week. Ken was elated. Without hesitation he accepted this stroke of good fortune and signed the contract. He was instructed to present himself back at the office in a couple of days when he would be issued with the keys and his rent book.

Ken bought some second-hand furniture just as the basic minimum that he and Ben would require to begin with at least. He read every word of the 'Items For Sale' classified advertisements in the local paper and acquired other essentials. He felt sure that by his actions so far his parents would see that he had taken his dad's ultimatum to heart and as such he reckoned if he was short of anything, he could borrow from his mam.

On the weekend before moving day all four of them, Albert, Mabel, Ken and Ben, went for a walk around the partly built Brookside Estate and located the new house. Brand new, and that he hadn't realised. There was a front garden and they walked up the garden path and peered through the windows.

'Very nicely decorated,' observed Mabel. 'I do like magnolia. You'll need some carpets though or maybe you can make do with lino and a few rugs?'

Ben and Albert meanwhile had disappeared around the back. There was a big garden although it was littered with builder's rubbish, brick rubble and the like. It would take a great deal of hard work before it looked like a garden and less like a bomb site.

'We'll get your dad to build a chicken run if you'd like that,' suggested Ben's grandad. Having seen the house and noted the close proximity to the school, a short walk across the fields, and to his grandparents' house, Ben was less apprehensive about moving in with his dad. In fact secretly, he was quite excited by the prospect. His own bedroom! He was looking forward to it.

Over the next few years everything went well. Albert kept

a close watch on his son and grandson and their relationship did develop as Albert had hoped. Stability and routine were re-established.

Chapter Twenty-Six

It was now four years that Ben and his dad had begun living together. And it had been together that they had cleared the back of the house and now had a productive vegetable garden, so much so that Ken was growing more than they needed and supplying his parents as well. Ben was in his final year at Grove Road Junior School and a model pupil according to the teacher Ken had met at parents' evening. Ben's piano playing was coming on as well although Ken couldn't quite see the point in that.

As Ben had got older his dad was relying on him much more for things like shopping and housekeeping. They were also spending less time together. Ben was becoming independent and wanted a bicycle. All of his schoolfriends had one.

'If you pass the 11-plus lad, I'll buy you a new one!'

Ben Blake pondered his dad's words for a few seconds.

'And what if I don't?'

'You'll get one second-hand from the classifieds you cheeky young bugger, or maybe we'll see what the newsagent has got advertised in the shop window. Be a bloody sight cheaper.'

Perhaps this was the incentive Ben needed. A second-hand bike? No way! Jamie, Ben's best mate at school, through the infants and now almost at the end of their time at the juniors, had recently been given a brand new one for no other reason than it was his birthday. But then Jamie's dad was loaded. He owned a hosiery wholesale business. He was the local Tory councillor who drove around in a Rover 100 and looked for all the world like the pompous git that Ken (and many others in the village) considered him to be.

Ben knew only too well that even if he did get the scholarship to the grammar school his dad would be hard pushed to buy the uniform, sports kit, geometry set (whatever that was) and everything else that he would be required to have, never mind a means of getting to the grammar school on a bike. As it was his dad, a single parent struggled to pay for his piano lessons. Could have been less of a struggle if he had spent less on booze perhaps? Still, Ben knew he was bright enough to pass the 11-plus. Mrs Owen, his teacher at the juniors, had told him often enough. And the academic and bookwork stuff came to him fairly easily anyway. He often had to explain things to his mate but it didn't seem fair that Jamie, rooted firmly in the 'B' stream at school could have whatever he wanted just by asking his old man for it.

'Ok,' Ben said, 'I'll do my best dad. I promise.' Ken knew he'd heard those words before somewhere.

'That's all I ask lad. I'll start saving. Your mother would have been proud if she hadn't have buggered off.' Ken realised that coming from him, reference to the boy's mother's disappearance was perhaps a little unfair.

Ben never really understood why his mother left when he was but a baby. Likewise had it really been necessary for his dad to dump him on to his parents, Ben's grandparents? He did know only too well that his dad had not had the opportunities that potentially he had now. It had become quite clear to Ben that his dad really wasn't cut out to be a single parent. He was a secondary modern kid whose parents hadn't been able to send him to the grammar school even though he was bright enough. And then he had been conscripted and sent off to war anyway. Not that Ben knew what his dad did in the war, it was obvious he fitted in with army life. He had risen through the ranks to become a sergeant. But what had happened after the war? Had there been some kind of trouble? Ben sometimes thought that his dad believed he was still in the army, barking orders, bullying and generally laying down the law. All of that he could take but he was not so placatable when it came to the physical violence he suffered on those occasions when his dad returned from the pub with a skin full.

He'd never really known his mother and often wished that she was there since he was sure she would moderate his dad's strict authoritarian regime. 'Spare the rod and spoil the child!' was his dad's maxim. Even so, and in general, Ben was anxious to please. He always made an effort to comply with instructions, to do as he was told, not wishing to incur his dad's wrath nor feel the back of his hand.

And so it was that life went on. With the 11-plus exam in the bag, a scholarship to the grammar school and a new bike, his dad's house rules remained unforgiving.

'Be home by six o'clock, or else! You seem to think you can treat this place like a hotel? I work hard to put food on the table...' Ben had heard it all before.

Months later, Ben and Jamie lay back on the railway embankment smoking the Player's Navy Cut that Jamie had nicked from the pompous councillor. Ben was thinking about the direction his life might take. Goodness knows what Jamie was thinking! Ben didn't see very much of Jamie these days. The grammar school's homework regime, helping his dad on the garden at weekends and piano practice meant that he only ever got to see Jamie during the school holidays. Becoming a proficient pianist had become Ben's ambition almost since his sixth birthday and for a year or so now, the paper-round he had from the newsagent's meant he could help out his dad by paying Miss Bedford the half-crown a week for lessons. Whilst his grandad had been in the army, he learned to play the piano and in consequence was much more sympathetic to Ben's musical aspirations. He regularly offered encouragement. His dad rarely did if at all. The piano was still in his grandparents' spare room and he went there to practise on most days. So on top of every-thing else he didn't have much time to spare. Just at that moment it seemed to Ben that Jamie's life had it all. Maybe he didn't have the prospects in the sense that Ben had but did that matter? Jamie's dad had money and a ready-made job for Jamie was assured when he left Eastfield Secondary Modern. He also had a mother and his dad was far from the disciplinarian Ben's dad was. Jamie's was a soft home-life and with a TV. It was all a piece of cake for Jamie. Ben looked at his new bike leaning against the fence and he wondered whether all the extra graft to get it had been worth it, particularly since he knew life was going to get harder. But then he was familiar with the 'grass is always greener' proverb.

This section of the railway embankment where bridge Number 80 crosses the Grand Union Leicester Line Canal and the LMS main railway line near Newton Harcourt had become a favourite spot. Ben and Jamie would often bike the ten miles or so to get there for no particular reason other than to collect train numbers. They might ride along the towpath for a while, fathom the mysteries of how a lock worked and marvel at the engineering before lying on the isolated slopes of the cutting and daydreaming. They didn't really speak to each other very much but somehow enjoyed each other's company. Jamie was developing his smoking habit and they would both check off train numbers in their Ian Allen trainspotting books. Occasionally they'd laugh at each other's jokes, and swap tales of misdeeds at school and of their respective teachers. But more often than not, what talk there was principally involved their fascination with girls. And especially with the bodies of the fairer sex and not necessarily from an aesthetic appreciation either. On this particular afternoon, Jamie was expounding on how boys' exploits or 'sexploits' with girls or 'birds' as they were commonly referred to especially at the secondary modern, were rated on a scoring system. Jamie explained,

'One point for a snog, two for groping outside the clothes, three for getting inside the bra, four for–' Just as the more intimate details were about to be revealed Black Five Number 45455 hauling eight coaches in LMS livery came thundering past on the up line to St Pancras. As the clouds of smoke and steam dissipated and with the decrescendo of the rhythmic clatter Ben became aware that his excitement with the passing express had not been shared by his mate. In fact, Jamie hadn't even paused in his discourse.

'–and ten points for going the whole way!" Ben could only wonder what qualified for four to nine points. And so it was with a stirring in his Y fronts that he reached for his pencil and his Ian Allen.

'Bugger!' he exclaimed.

'What's up?'

'I've already got it.'

'Got what?'

'45455.' They both convulsed into laughter.

'C'mon we'd better go home.'

Chapter Twenty-Seven

'Again!' squawked Miss Bedford. Her tone was such that Ben had little choice but to do as he was told. Twice already she'd rapped his knuckles with her ruler for getting his fingering wrong. Scales were one thing. Ben was fairly confident with them. But the arpeggios were giving him (and Miss Bedford) grief and the exam date loomed large on the calendar.

Ben's grandad had conspired with Miss Bedford to put Ben through the grade examinations of the Associated Board of the Royal Schools of Music; the examining body 'inspired by disinterested motives for the benefit of musical education'. Over the past couple of years, Ben's talent had developed under Miss Bedford's guidance. Some of Haydn's piano sonatas were easily within his grasp and he was playing regularly for school assembly. Sitting at the piano at the front of the hall was attracting a bit of 'pop star' attention from some of the girls, and providing a welcome distraction from the Headmaster, Mr Oldham's daily lectures. Ben had never really considered the grade exams as the route to becoming a proficient pianist, he just wanted to play. But, he supposed, they helped with his technique. This was evident from the fact that he had become accomplished to the extent that he had become the youngest pupil in the school ever to win the annual music prize. His music master at school, Mr Sims had pointed out to him that exam success was 'a distinction worthy of attainment' and which paved the way to music college.

Amongst Ben's admirers was Christina, a pretty girl with shoulder length auburn hair. With her shapely figure and 'a nice arse' according to Jamie, she certainly turned heads. Ben was becoming besotted and he and Tina were in each other's company on an increasingly regular basis much to Jamie's chagrin and possibly to the detriment of matters which should have been of a higher priority. They both had their O-levels coming up. Transition into the 6th form was dependent upon good grades in at least five O-levels. From there, A-level success would be the key to higher education, college and university establishments.

'Have you done your homework? You're not going out until you have! And don't think you can go swanning off with that girlfriend of yours at the weekend either. I've been keeping my eye on you and I know where you go and what you get up to. You've been seen by a mate of mine that uses the Old Greyhound at Great Glen. Don't know why you're wasting your time with that 'no-hope' mate of yours either; lad of your age collecting sodding train numbers! You've been seen by the cut at Newton. You'll end up like him if you're not careful. Your grandad tells me your piano practice has been slipping a bit as well. Oh, and by the way, if you're expecting any food on the table you'll need to get to the shops. I also want you to give me a hand in the garden.'

On it went. Like a long-playing record. But it was now becoming more relentless day by day. His dad was certainly stepping up the discipline and Ben was continually looking for whatever subterfuge he thought he might get away with to escape. With his O-levels just weeks away, he felt his revision schedule was compromised at home. It was always 'do this, do that, clear up, tidy your room'. He needed some peace and quiet with no interruptions from a drunkard of a father.

His Dad's attitude and behaviour softened just a little with the news that Ben had passed his grade 5 piano exam with distinction. He'd also gone on to score a maximum in the theory test. But Ben was now looking to increase his points score with Tina! On dates so far, he not yet got past four and his sap was rising. Blinkered by infatuation tinged with lust he'd given up the lessons with Miss Bedford, not that he'd told his dad who continued to shell out the two-and-six a week. Ben was now getting much more help from his music teacher at school, Mr Sims for whom he had greater respect. Miss Bedford had been an 'ok' teacher, if a bit of a tartar; a spinster of the old school. Mr Sims on the other hand delivered a much more progressive style of teaching both in terms of method and repertoire. The money saved on Miss Bedford's lessons Ben misappropriated and put it towards 'going out' as was the phrase given to teenage relationships. As soon as the exams season was over Ben was planning to take Tina on a 'special date' – a bike ride – to Newton Harcourt, and not to spot train numbers either.

Chapter Twenty-Eight

Life aboard *Emily Rose* was leisurely and unhurried; completely stress free. Compared to the only other working-life Helen had known as a land-army girl toiling on Frank's farm, this buying and selling was almost as she imagined being on holiday would be. Boats worked their way up and down the Foxton Flight. She became friends with many of the boatpeople. Nearly every night was a party night in the Foxton Locks Inn and Jock was the life and soul of the party. Thanks to Fred and the 'arrangement' between he and Jock, *Emily Rose* was moored in prime position. She was virtually on the pub's doorstep. And it wasn't just the boatpeople who were always after a bargain. During the warmer weather especially, Foxton was a tourist attraction and ramblers, cyclists, miscellaneous sightseers and visitors with cars supplemented the well-established client base.

When 'running the shop' as Jock referred to it was less busy and Helen had time on her hands she had taken to decorating *Emily Rose* in the traditional style with roses and castles. Not just the boat itself but its many fixtures and fittings as well. On winter evenings when there was no action in the pub Helen would sit in the armchair in the cabin making fancy lace doilies or devising space saving features that would afford them a little more room. If there was a downside to on-board life it would have to be the cramped conditions in the cabin. The lack of basic 'facilities' was one the boat's less endearing features too. The 'thunder-box' and tin bath at Rosemary and Neville's old house were almost a luxury by comparison to the 'bucket and chuck it' method.

Helen's relationship with Jock hadn't progressed in quite the way Jock had hoped and although they shared the bed Helen had not given in to any of his persuasive flattery even when in a state of inebriation. The fruit that Jock was hoping to taste remained forbidden. Ken had been her first love and for all that he had mistreated her, subjected her to mental and physical abuse and subsequently abandoned her, he was the father of her child. In quiet moments of reflection she knew in her heart that she still loved him and hoped that one day they would be reconciled and reunited despite her assertions that she never wanted to see him again.

Helen thought of Ben now and again and wondered what sort of boy he was turning into now he was nearly seven. How was he coping living with his grandparents? How was he getting on at school? At least she had honoured her pledge to sponsor his upkeep.

Now and again and by way of a change of scenery they would take the *Emily Rose* on the Market Harborough Arm. An evening in the Black Horse or the Shoulder of Mutton in Foxton village was always a welcome treat. For new clothes, medicines, books or other requisites that were hard to come by on the canal, Market Harborough was much more of a proper town with bigger shops, a pharmacy, library, hardware store, and shops for pretty much everything they had ever needed. Helen always remembered to get Ben's birthday card and money order in Market Harborough. Sometimes it was easier to leave the boat tied up and take a trip to town on the Ariel.

All things considered Helen was happy. She was making

a small fortune and had opened an account with the Market Harborough Building Society. However she knew it would soon be time to move on. It was the height of the summer. Foxton Locks was heaving with tourists. Business from the *Emily Rose* had been brisk to the extent that stocks of everything would soon be exhausted at the rate they were selling. Since all rationing had ended virtually everything was readily available from regular outlets although one would expect to pay the recommended retail price. The black market as such had become a thing of the past and it was now nigh on impossible for Jock to acquire merchandise at a sufficiently low price which he in turn could sell for a profit. Jock's East End contacts had gone to ground or prison and it had dawned on him that the risks he was taking dealing with stolen goods were now much greater, almost to the point of being unacceptable compared to how things were when his enterprise was in its infancy.

It was time to take stock; time to move on. Jock could sense that Helen had had enough and needed a change. They had both made a lot of money and their staying in one place compounded the risk of being investigated. They were after all trading illegally without a licence. And the goods they were trading? All illicitly obtained if not actually stolen. Helen and Jock had a 'directors" meeting the outcome of which was that they would leave Foxton and make their way back to Kilby Wharf.

Chapter Twenty-Nine

School was out. Examinations had been completed and passed or failed. Time would tell and there was no point in worrying or speculating now. The long summer holiday held exciting possibilities. The 'special date', the day they'd been looking forward to, had finally arrived. The sun was shining and it was pleasantly warm. They met as prearranged. In secret, boyfriend and girlfriend. As they pushed their bicycles down the road from the Red Lion, Ben couldn't avert his gaze from Tina in her shorts and flimsy blouse.

'You look lovely Tina!' remarked Ben. Not in a flattering sort of way but with all the respect and deference that he could muster given the quivering state of embarrassment he was in. Tina blushed with a demure coyness but her body language said all that Ben wanted to hear and she was well aware of what it was saying as well! And off they went.

The minor roads had very little traffic and allowed them to ride two abreast chatting away about everything in general and nothing in particular. After an hour or so and a couple of stops to drink some of the water that Ben had thought to bring in his saddlebag, they were able to leave the road and access the canal towpath at the Little Glen Bridge. They both delighted in the tranquillity. With barely a ripple of the water and the sunlight dappling through the trees, it was blissful. The only sounds were birdsong and Tina softly humming to herself. Ben was loving every second. Miles away from the garden, from the piano and from his dad. They sauntered on pushing their bikes, exchanging embarrassed glances and smiling a lot.

As they approached Kilby Bridge there were narrow-boats moored by the banks and the peace and quiet was momentarily disturbed by the characteristic and rhythmic 'thumpy-thumpy-thumpy' of a traditional Bolinder diesel engine accompanied by the little synchronised puffs of exhaust from the chimney as a narrowboat boat gently passed by on its way to who knows where. They gave the boatman a little wave. He returned their greeting with a smile and a look which said, 'There's a lucky boy!'

By the time they reached bridge Number 87 it was almost lunchtime and already there were a few customers sitting outside the Navigation Inn at Kilby Bridge. Although he was underage Ben felt emboldened by the occasion and went into the pub and emerged triumphantly a few moments later with two halves of shandy and a packet of salted crisps. They sat in silence and enjoyed their refreshment watching the various comings and goings on and off the canal. In the distance one could hear the occasional rushes of steam as trains urged on their way up to St Pancras or down to Sheffield.

'Shall we go a little further?' Ben enquired. 'There's Newton Harcourt just a bit further on, it's not that far.' Ben and Jamie had often wandered the short distance from their favourite spot by the railway and over the bridge. There by St Luke's Church was yet another idyllic spot where one could lie on a bed of leaves and needles amongst the gravestones and with only the sound of occasional railway traffic, completely lose oneself in rambling thought or fall asleep at the drop of a pinecone. Ben told Tina how several months earlier in response to Jamie being short on ideas he had suggested that Jamie's history project could be about St Luke's Church. Maybe include a few gravestones or brass rubbings. Whether the project was ever completed and handed in he had no idea. Ben hadn't seen Jamie for some time and according to his dad, Jamie was a 'no-hoper' and had 'gone off the rails'.

Anyway, whilst he would have been happy to show her the sights such as they were Ben had other things on his mind and Tina knew it. He had previously found the church interesting, and he was sure Tina would do likewise but today was not the day! Thinking back to Jamie's project fleetingly, he recalled some of the history and particularly fascinated by the organ.

The guided tour was cut short by mutual consent and, they crossed the bridge Number 80 towards his favourite place, the spot by the railway that Ben had always intended should be their destination. But as they drew closer what was this? Laughing and horsing around drinking bottles of beer and smoking there of all people was Jamie. There were some other lads and girls from Eastfield as well. Whilst Ben and Jamie had always got on together more often than not there was an uncomfortable friction between the grammar school and secondary modern kids. Neither Ben nor Tina required any explanation as to what the party on the embankment had been up to and Ben couldn't help but wonder how many points had been scored! Even so he was not amused to say the least. His plan was thwarted. He hurriedly steered Tina back towards the canal before they were spotted. He was anxious to avoid any confrontation, embarrassment or anything else which would totally ruin the day if indeed it hadn't been spoiled already.

Ben hastily devised a 'Plan B' and he and Tina continued into Newton Harcourt village and cycled off towards Great

Glen. They didn't notice the narrowboat making its way towards the Newton Top Lock Number 23 and onwards towards Leicester. Decorated in traditional style, it was the *Emily Rose*. On the tiller was a short fellow, and standing in the companionway, a woman.

Ben and Tina were well on their way towards Great Glen and so they didn't notice the man with the beard on the lockside at Number 24. They wouldn't have noticed him step aboard the *Emily Rose* nor would they have heard the argument that then ensued between the boatman and the man with the beard. They wouldn't have noticed the woman attempting to conciliate. Ben and Tina were close to the junction with the main A6 road from Market Harborough to Leicester when the *Emily Rose* disappeared into lock Number 25. They wouldn't have been aware of the fight between the boatman and man with the beard. They would not have heard the commotion, the shouting and cursing nor the splash as the man with the beard was hit over the head with the windlass key and pushed overboard into the lock.

When they arrived at Great Glen, Ben went into the shop, just up the road from the Old Greyhound pub. He bought some chocolate and a bottle of lemonade which he put in his saddlebag – refreshments for later on!

They mounted their bikes and peddled off back towards Newton Middle lock, the so-called 'Spinney' lock and under Wain Bridge not stopping until they reached the Top Half-Mile lock, Number 25, next to Flaxman's Spinney. This is isolated enough thought Ben. Breathing heavily from the exertion of the ride down the towpath and in anticipation he apologised.

'Sorry about all that Tina, but I'm desperate for a pee.' And off he disappeared into the spinney. Just as he was buttoning up, the tranquillity was split wide open by an ear-piercing scream. He rushed back towards the lock and there was Tina, absolutely distraught, alternately sobbing and shrieking whilst pointing into the lock. Ben looked and immediately saw the cause of Tina's hysterics.

'Is he dead?' she wept. Ben had turned pale. He knelt down to get a closer look at the body floating face down in the lock. The corpse looked somehow familiar. Then he noticed the bike lying on the towpath. Not his own, his dad's!

'We need to get help', he trembled. Then as if panicked and displaying a characteristic he had not previously witnessed Tina was on her bike and off like a startled rabbit back up the towpath towards St Luke's Church.

Supressing a lapse into 'headless chicken' mode Ben's logical and practical common sense kicked in. He reckoned that if he opened the paddles on the top gates the lock would fill and float the body to the top of the lock where it would be much easier to recover. As fate would have it a windlass key for the winding gear was there and he started to crank the windlass for all he was worth. At first there was a trickle as the cast-iron paddle slowly lifted. The trickle very quickly became a torrent. The surge of water rolled the body over. Ben looked back and any doubt he may have had was instantly dispelled; all hope dashed. It was his dad. Howling in despair he lost concentration; forgot what he was doing. The pawl on the winding gear disengaged from the cog. The windlass became uncontrollable, spinning violently as the weight of the paddle caused the rack to slam down. As it did so Ben's hand was trapped between the rack and pinion. The pain was excruciating. He roared in agony. Literally, his hand had become impaled 'on the rack' and crushed to a bloody pulp. Ben lost consciousness and fell by the side of the lock with his right arm in the air, his hand trapped and totally mutilated. Much later Ben came to in the unfamiliar surroundings of an emergency room at Leicester Royal Infirmary. His hand was heavily bandaged with his hand and arm suspended above him; not unlike the position they were in when he passed out. There was severe bruising to his abdomen where the whirling windless had hit him and the pain was intense. He was assured by a nurse that it would ease with the morphine injection he'd been given.

Lying there in agony, self-pity and loathing in equal measure he knew that if there had been any prospect of music college and becoming a professional pianist, it was down the toilet now. And in many ways it was his own fault. Ben tortured himself.

'Why, oh why, oh why?' His sufferance and self-pity were greater than he could endure. He had to admit that it was a case of 'dad knew best'?

'I should have listened!' If ever he needed a shoulder to cry on now was the time. There was desperation in his crying.

Apparently without giving any consideration for her own wellbeing it had been Tina who had affected the rescue. Having shot off up the towpath back to Newton Church bridge she had managed to persuade Jamie and his mates to come to the rescue and after they had extricated Ben's hand from the winding gear the ambulance which Tina had telephoned from the kiosk at Newton had arrived.

Chapter Thirty

Had it not been for the noise of a passing train carried on the wind Helen's scream would have been heard for miles. Jock had never made such a rapid exit from a lock. He pushed the throttle to full ahead, the Russell Newbery roared and *Emily Rose* surged forward. Helen's fury was raging. She flew at Jock flailing her arms and punching, apoplectic with anger. Jock did his best to fend off the blows. Had the boat been closer to the bank Helen would surely have jumped off and gone back to the lock Number 25. At the speed the boat was travelling, creating a wake which was washing over the banks on both sides, they were soon at the Bottom Half Mile Number 26. Helen leaped from the boat and ran back along the towpath towards Number 25. Jock shouted after her but she was too intent on returning to the scene of Jock's crime, the murder of the bearded man; Ken.

Jock manoeuvred the boat with difficulty in the lock. He was trembling, not only from Helen's attack but the deranged and disordered reasoning behind the accusations which had led to the fight with Ken. Having been beaten in a fight with Ken on a previous occasion Jock was not about to suffer another malicious offensive at the hands of Ken's hysterical frenzy again. The windlass key was within his grasp in a bracket on the stern rail. He'd grabbed it and with as much force as he could draw upon he had struck Ken on the head and pushed him overboard and into the lock.

In the nightly sessions with George and other locals at the bar of the Old Greyhound talk was of cheap wines, spirits, tobacco, watches, cameras, all manner of stuff, or so it was rumoured, that could be bought from a narrowboat generally moored at Foxton. Ken had put two and two together and decided to check out the rumours by going to Foxton. A brief glimpse of Jock on the quay was all that was needed. The rumours were confirmed. There were certain issues between them that required resolving. The sight of Helen emerging from the cabin was not what he was expecting and his intentions to have it out with Jock were intensified tenfold. Ken was overcome with a protective possessiveness. Memories of the love and the intimacy he and Helen had shared came flooding back. Ken found it impossible to accept that despite the intervening years Helen was now with another man. He was bitterly disappointed and almost out of his mind with jealousy. Would Helen really have committed adultery with Jock? Now there were two issues to resolve. But here and now were neither the time nor the place.

It had been a complete coincidence that Ken should have been down by the canal as the *Emily Rose* was approaching that lock. He had merely gone for a walk to try and put together a confrontational strategy. Stepping aboard when the boat entered the lock was a completely impulsive act and he immediately lost his composure before broaching either of his claims. Ken was intent on recovering his share of the black market dealings and equally adamant that he would reclaim his wife and make every effort to achieve a reconciliation.

Jock left the boat sitting in lock Number 26 and walked back to find Helen kneeling beside Number 25, sobbing. He knew there was little point in trying to console her. It had been obvious to him for a long time that Helen was still in love with her husband for all that he had wronged her and the manner in which she had been abused and mistreated.

Eventually he persuaded her to return to the boat. They would go to Kilby Wharf and decide what to do from there. They worked the boat together, in silence apart from Helen's muted sobbing. When they arrived at Kilby Helen gave serious thoughts about walking to Ernie's farm. Would Ernie and Kate still be there? What would their reaction be to seeing Helen after all this time? 'Too many unknowns,' she told herself. So, for all that it would be difficult, if not unbearable, she decided to stay put for a day or so and work on an escape plan.

Jock could not decide on the direction in which his future lay so *Emily Rose* stayed at the wharf. After thrashing the Russell Newbery in the way that he had Jock thought he should give the engine a little care and attention; change the oil, the impeller, the filters and such; all routine maintenance which had been sadly neglected. Spare parts had to be ordered to carry out the engine service and they took a long time in coming.

It was on a Friday lunchtime a couple of weeks later that Jock was alerted by something of a clamour. Folk who had been sitting outside the Navigation Inn were lining themselves on either side of lock 30, Kilby Lock. Sightseers were also crowded on to bridge 82. A boat was coming up. Competition from the road transport and the railways had diminished significantly since the war to the point where there were very few working boats left. The opportunity to watch a real narrowboat laden with whatever it might be carrying work its way through the lock was something of a novelty and always drew a crowd.

As the boat came into view as it passed beneath the

bridge. Jock was able to make out that it was *The Damselfly*. If it was, then the *Mayfly* wouldn't be that far behind. *Damselfly* worked her way through the lock and came to lay alongside *Emily Rose* whilst waiting for the *Mayfly*. The boatman troubled Jock for a purchase and bought one of the last cartons of hand-rolling tobacco that Jock had and handed over the cash.

'I got the *'inckley Times* 'ere, if yo' wan' a read.'

'Aye, cheers mate,' and there was some boatman banter between the two of them. As *Mayfly* cleared the lock, both boats set off in close order.

Jock sat on an empty beer-crate on the canal bank and idly flicked through the paper. Something in it caught his eye. Helen's escape plan still hadn't been finalised but she and Jock were at least speaking again.

'Helen, Helen, where are ye lass? Come quick.'

Helen appeared from below on the boat.

'Ye better come and take a look.'

She climbed onto the bank and peered over Jock's shoulder to see what had stirred him up. He'd been looking at the Public Notices page and there in the obituaries column Helen also spotted the cause of the fuss.

The death is announced of Sergeant Kenneth Robert Blake (32) late of the Seaforth Highlanders. Son of Albert and Mabel Blake, father of Ben. The funeral will take place at St Catherine's Church at mid-day on Friday 23rd August.

So, the body had been recovered from the lock.

Helen instantly burst into tears and was distressed all over again.

'Och, c'mon the noo Helen love. Dinnae upset yoursel'.'

But upset she was and no mistake. Any number of attempts to console her were to no avail.

She retreated to the boat and lay on the bed sobbing her heart out for the rest of the day.

After several days of grieving Helen announced that she wanted to go to funeral. Jock announced that he didn't but he agreed to take Helen on the Ariel and drop her off at the church. Jock's unwillingness to attend the funeral became a very sore point. Helen insisted that he should accompany her. It was the very least he could do. She reminded Jock that after all, he and Ken had been schoolfriends, comrades in arms and business partners. She was almost prepared to accept his contention that he had acted in self-defence. However, self-defence or not Helen insisted that he should seek atonement with a visit to church; that it would be good for his soul. But for all her pleading and insistence Jock was adamant. He would not attend and that was it.

During the few days before the funeral, there was no love lost between them. Helen decided she was leaving once and for all. She declined to accept Jock's offer of a lift on the motorbike in favour of booking a taxi and on the 23rd August, she packed a bag with a few clothes, her building society passbook, the sentimental possessions she had on the boat, including a 35mm camera for her Uncle Sid and, of course her biscuit tin. The taxi took her to her sister Rosemary's house.

Chapter Thirty-One

'I've examined your hand and, there are no two ways about it, it's a mess!' Ben had been dozing intermittently despite the pain and the discomfort of the position he was in with his arm suspended. A doctor accompanied by a nurse was now talking to him whilst looking at x-ray photographs at the same time. 'X-rays?' thought Ben, he had absolutely no recollection of any x-rays having been taken.

'I'm Mr Courtenay, one of the members of the Hand Surgery team here. From our first assessment a physical examination and the x-rays it would appear that you have intra-articular fractures, significant damage to the soft tissue and you have severed the flexor tendons to your fore and middle fingers'. Ben didn't really have much idea of what the doctor was talking about. He wasn't rating his bedside manner very highly either. All he knew for sure right at that moment was that it bloody well hurt like hell and was throbbing like a bastard.

'How does it feel?' Mr Courtenay enquired, almost in a matter of fact manner, devoid of any sympathy.

'It bloody well hurts like hell and is throbbing like a bastard,' Ben blurted, realising at the same time that perhaps he had no need to swear but needed to make the emphasis.

'Hardly surprising,' responded the doctor stating the obvious, Ben thought.

'The fractures we can mend. Should be quite straight-forward. But you will require surgery otherwise there is no prospect of your regaining any movement in those two fingers. How old are you?'

'Sixteen, nearly seventeen.'

'The young lady that came with you in the ambulance, she your sister?'.

Momentarily the pain in his hand gave way to a different pain, a torment even, as the tears came.

'I don't have a sister.'

Mr Courtenay gave Ben a sideways look.

'Can we contact your mother?'

'I don't know where she is,' sobbed Ben.

'Who's your next of kin, your dad? Can we contact you dad then?'

'I, I, I don't have one any more,' stammered Ben as he realised the full implications of what had happened in the previous few hours. He related the drama that had been played out at Top Half-Mile lock.

'Well, we'll need to contact your next of kin.' Did this doctor not understand the gravity of the tragedy just described to him?

'That'll be my grandad then.' The tears now streaming uncontrollably. With little more than, 'Hmm, I see', Mr Courtenay walked off and was replaced at the bedside by the nurse.

'Hello Ben,' whispered the nurse. 'I'm Carol and I'll be taking care of you.' She gave Ben a smile. Carol's softly spoken, maternal manner was something of a comfort and Ben accepted the tissue she offered him.

'What will surgery entail?' asked Ben, clearly anxious.

'You'll be given a general anaesthetic and the surgeon will probably have to enlarge that nasty cut across your palm to locate the ends of the tendons which he'll then stitch together. Depending on the configuration of the broken bones they will probably have to be pinned or wired to hold them in the right position whilst they mend. Your hand and arm will then be in a plaster cast for between six and eight weeks.'

The whole procedure and the timescale seemed impossible to Ben and the tears started again.

'C'mon now,' said Carol, 'it'll mend, don't worry. It's difficult to predict the final outcome as there are so many variables with hand surgery. But Mr Courtenay is one of the best hand surgeons in the country and after physiotherapy I'm sure you'll be playing the piano again'.

'How did you know I play...' he corrected himself, '... played the piano?' asked Ben, drying his eyes.

'Your girlfriend told me – silly me, I almost forgot to mention, she's here to see you. Shall I fetch her in?'

Ben thanked Carol and with another smile she was gone. Seconds later Tina appeared at his bedside.

'I can't stay long. Dad's waiting in the car for me.' She briefly examined the tips of the fingers of his right hand, swollen with bruising. Black, tinged with yellow and purple just protruding from the dressing. She shuddered.

'Mum says if there's anything you need, clean clothes maybe, your washbag, anything at all just let me know. We'll help you get through this.'

Holding back the tears as best he could he just wanted to hug and hold on to her for ever.

'I'm so very sorry,' Ben said. 'It was supposed to be our perfect day out and it should never have ended like this.'

'I know, I know. Never mind. We'll have our perfect day out before too long.'

'Never mind? Easier than it seems!' Ben's response was laden with sarcasm. His hand was alternately aching and throbbing, The two of them sat looking at each other and she held his left hand. No words were spoken for several minutes until eventually Tina got up.

Hesitatingly, she reached across the bed and kissed him.

'I really have to go now but I'll come and visit tomorrow if you like. Don't forget to let us know if there's anything you want. I hope the pain eases. Night night.' And as she blew him another kiss, she was gone.

Ben lay wondering what on earth Tina had said to her parents. The whole day out was supposed to have been a secret and he hoped she hadn't got into trouble for being deceitful. Then his mind suddenly conjured up the mental image of his dad sitting by the shed in the garden at home. In an instant this scene was eclipsed by the vision of the body in the lock. A torrent of thoughts surged into his head. Why had he not been open and up-front? Why did his dad not trust him? Was there really a need for his dad to follow him, to check up on him? Had he been drinking in the Old Greyhound? Was he drunk? Had he fallen off his bike into the lock? Where was his dad's body now? Had someone recovered his bike? What was to be done about a funeral? Has anyone told his grandparents? So many questions. And before long he drifted into a fitful sleep.

Chapter Thirty-Two

Ben spent the next week in the Royal Infirmary. After the swelling had reduced sufficiently he had the first of the operations required to repair the damage to his hand. As he came round after the general anaesthetic, he recognised Carol sitting beside his bed but he had no idea where he was.

'How do you feel?' asked Carol.

'Where am I?' mumbled Ben

'We've moved you out of the emergency room and onto the general men's ward.'

'Oh' was the only response Ben could manage.

'I'll bring you a cup of tea in a little while.'

Ben tried to move his right arm, but it was somehow immobilised. The pain was different and much less intense that it had been. He could see that a needle had been inserted into his arm which in turn was connected to a tube leading to a bottle of colourless liquid on a chrome stand by the bed. He felt very drowsy and drifted off to sleep.

When he awoke, the ward was busy with quite a clamour as nurses served trays of food from trolleys to other patients up and down the ward. Ben had no idea what time it was but took a calculated guess at tea-time. He was hungry but, from the smells which were pervading the atmosphere, not sure he fancied whatever it was on offer. A nurse approached the foot of his bed.

'You're awake then.'

The manner in which she spoke didn't quite convey whether this was a question or merely a statement of the obvious. Ben wasn't sure. Whichever, her tone, like that of the doctor, conveyed no sympathy at all and he took an instant dislike to this particular angel of mercy. He decided to say nothing.

'You're only allowed some dry toast. I'll go and get it for you.'

'Thank you,' Ben said when the burnt offering was delivered.

'How long do I have to stay in here?' he wondered under his breath. It seemed she'd heard him as the officious nurse responded, 'Mr Courtenay will be round in the morning. He'll let you know.'

Ben was woken at some unearthly hour of the morning and invited to use the toilet. There were alternatives. He could pee in a bottle or use bedpan. He accepted the former of the options although it was a bit awkward connected to the drip with his right arm strapped across his chest. When he returned to his bed he was relieved to see Carol was on duty rather than the dragon lady from the previous day.

'Good morning Ben. You look much better than you did a couple of days ago. Hop into bed and I'll fetch you some breakfast. Scrambled egg ok?'

After breakfast had been cleared away, there began a hustle and bustle as nurses began straightening, tidying, and generally fussing over everything. The fellow in the next bed looked over towards Ben and offered an explanation.

'Matron's round,' he said as he sat nodding in an attempt to appear knowledgeable as if the explanation could justify the panic which had the nurses running around all aflutter.

'Oh,' said Ben as if he understood what this meant.

Then the doors at the end of the ward swung open and the ample yet stately figure of Matron glided into view followed by an entourage of various other members of the hospital staff. Matron barely gave Ben a second glance as the medical miscellany swept passed the end of his bed. 'Now you see it, now you don't,' thought Ben as he was reminded of a time he had 'spotted' a Pacific Class thunder by his vantage point on the Newton embankment.

As the excitement abated and the ward returned to a more relaxed level of activity Mr Courtenay, Carol and a couple of others in white coats who Ben took to be student doctors, gathered around his bed.

'I think the operation was successful. How does it feel?' And then he was gone before Ben had chance to speak.

After a short while Carol and one of the other white coats returned.

'We managed to locate the ends of your flexor tendons and stitch them together. At the same time we realigned the fractured digits and were able to wire them together. The wires are inserted through the skin and if all goes well, we can remove them in a month or so. Your hand will feel numb for a while and then you'll start to get pins and needles. That's a good sign letting you know that healing is taking place. We'll get you plastered in a day or so and then you can go home.'

'Plastered' was an apt description of the state his dad got into especially on a Friday night and Ben reflected that not only would his life be different from now but how his dad would be missed by all his mates, the 'good old boys' at 'The Cross Keys'.

After they'd gone Ben thought about what he'd been told and for the first time since the incident at the lock he felt a little more cheerful. After tea which consisted of some kind of poached white fish in milk with over-boiled cabbage and mash and which despite not looking appetising didn't actually taste too bad, the doors at the end of the ward were wedged open – the sign that visiting time was about to start. There was a bit of rush as friends and relatives came in bearing bags and bunches of flowers, anxiously seeking out whoever it was they'd come to visit. As Ben watched, a mother and a couple of kids settled by the chap in the next bed down the ward. The mother gave Ben a smile. He hadn't noticed he too had a visitor.

'Hello Ben'. It was Tina and he couldn't recollect ever being so pleased to see anyone. She was clutching a small duffel bag in one hand which Ben recognised as his own.

'I went around to see your grandad and the police had already told him what had happened. He suggested that we went to your house and get you some stuff – I love your pyjamas,' she giggled. Ben wasn't sure whether he was embarrassed or not.

'Got you some clean underpants as well.' Now as he blushed, of his embarrassment there was no doubt! Tina continued to lay out the contents of the duffel bag at the foot of the bed.

'What's in the shopping bag?' Ben enquired.

'Brought you some grapes and a copy of the latest *Railway Magazine*.'

'Did grandad say anything about... about...' Ben hesitated, but Tina knew exactly to what he was referring.

'There has to be an inquest and nothing can be done about a funeral until the coroner releases the body. It seems the police are involved. They think the death was suspicious and there may have to be an investigation when they know the cause.'

'Oh dear,' muttered Ben as he fiddled with the drip in his arm.

'Anyway, your grandad can tell you more about that. He should be here in a second – he's just buying Mr Sims a pint. He brought us over in his car.'

'Mr Sims? Blimey!'

Ben was one of Mr Sims most talented pupils and his music teacher had clearly been made aware of recent events. Ben's chain of thought reverted to his music and his doomed career. When, just as he was about to slide back into the slough of despond his grandad arrived.

'Now then lad!'

The three of them, Ben, Albert and Tina, sat talking for the next fifty minutes and before they knew it the bell rang to signify visiting time over.

Chapter Thirty-Three

On his next visit Albert had brought Mabel with him and they found Ben looking much more like himself sitting in the armchair next to his bed. Ben moved and sat on the bed so that his Grandma could sit in the chair.

'How're you doing lad?' Albert enquired. 'You're certainly looking a lot better.'

Ben's arm was no longer strapped across his chest. His hand and arm were encased in a plaster of Paris cast up to the elbow and supported in a sling. Just the tips of his fingers were visible.

'It's not so bad now Grandad. At least I can get up and walk about a bit when the Sister's not looking. I'll be glad to get out of here though. These old blokes don't half snore and fart.'

'Tell me about it!' exclaimed Mabel.

They all laughed.

Albert produced a brown Manila envelope from his waistcoat pocket.

'This was addressed to your dad but I think we know what it is.' Immediately the air was charged with nervous anticipation.

'Shall I open it?' he asked as he stood and opened it anyway.

'I expect it's my exam results,' surmised Ben.

'It's your exam results,' said Albert.

'That's what he said,' Mabel remonstrated. After a moment or two of studying the contents of the envelope Grandad looked at Ben in a teasing sort of way,

'Do you want to read them for yourself or shall I announce them out loud to the ward?' He laughed – a proper belly-laugh this time and handed the result sheet to his grandson.

English Language – A
English Literature – A
Mathematics – B
Latin – C
Geography – B
History – A
Music – A
Art – A

The initial grin on Ben's face gradually spread into a broad smile from ear to ear and he started giggling. He closed his eyes, raised his face to the ceiling and punched the air with a clenched fist – his left one naturally.

'Yes!'

'Yes indeed!' His grandma stood up and gave him a hug as best she could with his arm in a sling and everything.

'Fantastic!' whooped Ben.

'Well done, bloody well done lad!' exclaimed Albert.

'Clever boy,' added Mabel.

The round of applause that followed was augmented by Mr Courtenay, the white coats, Carol and another couple of nurses who were making their rounds.

'Well done, young man,' said Mr Courtenay. 'Five A's, 2 B's and a C, a fine effort by anyone's standard. I'm sure your parents will be delighted.' The metaphorical clanger was louder than any dropped bedpan. Carol whispered into Mr

Courtenay's ear whilst everyone else's open-mouthed stare witnessed his normal pallid complexion slowly rubricate to a shade of vermillion.

'Ah, sorry about that.' Mr Courtenay's embarrassment was apparent for all to see and the nurses started quietly tut-tutting.

'Anyway, I'm sure you'll be pleased to hear, you can go home tomorrow.'

With that, Mr Courtenay sloped off hoping the ground would open up and swallow him.

Albert could always be relied upon to recharge any atmosphere with some levity.

'He might be a good doctor but he's a daft bugger if ever I met one!'

The congratulatory gathering dispersed at the ringing of the bell and Ben was left alone to contemplate what might happen next. He had overcome the second major challenge in his education and the twists and turns in the uncertain road to his future were straightening out. That evening Albert forsook the Cross Keys and biked to the neighbouring village of Sapcote in favour of the Red Lion where he vaguely knew the landlord, Dennis who, he'd discovered, was Tina's dad.

And so it was that the following day Ben was discharged as an inpatient, given a prescription for some painkillers, should he need them, and an appointment card to return as an outpatient a few weeks hence. Sitting in the reception area of the hospital he wasn't quite sure how he was going to get home. He hadn't got more than a few shillings in his pocket and it hadn't previously occurred to him that perhaps he should have made some arrangements with his grandad. As it happened grandad had it all in hand. His visit to the Red Lion last night clearly had a purpose other than a couple of pints.

Sitting in Dennis' Ford Anglia Ben didn't quite know what to say. It was the first time he'd met Tina's dad and he was finding it all a bit intimidating.

'So, Ben, is it?'

'Yes sir,' came Ben's response whilst wondering who else he thought it might have been sitting with his daughter in the back of his car.

'I'm taking you to Albert's, I mean your grandad's house, is that right?'

'Thank you sir.'

Tina gave Ben a squeeze and a smile and in whispered tones throughout the journey, they compared their respective exam results. Tina's results were as good as Ben's.

Lunch at his grandparents' consisted of a doorstep cheese and pickle sandwich and a cup of tea. Mabel was fussing about like a mother hen and clearly irritating Albert who was trying to read the paper.

'Leave the lad be for goodness sake Mabel!'

Ben was feeling awkward about being there and was about to make an excuse for leaving when his grandad reached over to the mantelpiece for a letter filed behind the carriage clock.

'I've had this from the coroner's office,' he said. 'Apparently the verdict on your dad's death was 'misadventure'. The cause of death was trauma to the head consistent with his head hitting something or being struck with a blunt object. I'm not sure what any of this means and I've been scratching my head since the letter arrived yesterday, haven't I Mabel?" The question was rhetorical.

'I mean did he fall, did he jump, was he pushed, did he drown, had he been knocked out and chucked in the lock? It's a bloody mystery and that's for sure. Still at least we can now go ahead and make some arrangements for the funeral.'

'Can you help me grandad?' Ben was clearly distressed.

'Of course we will lad. Don't you worry, the undertaker'll do most of it for us anyway.'

Mabel sat in the armchair quietly weeping into her handkerchief.

Chapter Thirty-Four

Ben walked the short distance back to the new council estate where he and his dad had lived since just before his seventh birthday It was a fairly typical estate house, semi-detached, two bedrooms, an outhouse and well cared for garden with a shed. It used to be surrounded by fields but gradually the estate was extending as more and more new houses went up. As he was letting himself in, he noticed the outhouse door was not properly closed. On investigation he discovered that both his and his dad's bikes had been returned. That was something at least. He had wondered what might have happened to them.

The house was just as he had left it on 'that' day. There were items of mail and some other bits lying on the front doormat which he collected as he went into the sitting room; the front room as it was referred to. He closed the curtains. He wasn't sure why but he seemed to recall somebody telling him once that it was what people did when there had been a bereavement in the household. He sat on the sofa and looked through the post, nothing of any great interest, a gas bill, a Littlewoods coupon, a reminder from the milkman that he wanted paying on Friday this week. Poor Ben. All alone and without a clue. He heard a car pull up in the street outside. Then there came a knock at the front door. Nobody he knew knocked the front door; they all came to the back. He opened the door and there stood Jamie. A Triumph Herald convertible was parked by the front gate.

'What-ho Ben! Didn't know whether you'd be in, what with the curtains drawn.' He nodded in the direction of Ben's plastered arm still suspended in the sling. 'How is it?'

Ben invited Jamie in. The last time he'd seen Jamie albeit from a distance was on 'that' day. And not for the first time Ben's mind flashed back and again he relived the moments before he passed out.

'I brought your bike back and your dad's. Did you see?'

'Yes, thanks for that and thanks for what you did, you know, getting my hand out and everything.'

'No worries mate. Looked pretty nasty.' Ben related the nature of the injury, the treatment he'd had so far and his week in hospital. Before too long they were chatting away like the best friends they used to be.

'You still seeing Tina? Jamie asked.

'Sure am,' replied Ben. 'I think I'm in love,' he confessed. 'She's lovely.'

'Isn't she just. She was a real star, a heroine, the day of the...you know.

Jamie explained how Tina had galvanised him and his mates on the embankment at Newton into action.

'There was no panic, she just took control and gave the orders. Brilliant really. I always thought she was a bit stuck-up but I was wrong' Jamie admitted. The off-chance visit by Jamie had clearly cheered Ben up.

" 'When you're up to it, we can all go for a spin in the motor if you like. You and Tina, me and Diane.'

'Not Diane... her with the big...?'

'Oh, you know her then? Yes, that's her,' interrupted Jamie. 'We've been going steady for nearly three weeks now,' he announced proudly.

'Is that yours then, the Triumph?'

'It will be on my birthday. Dad's bought it for me. I've got the 'L' plates on but I'm not supposed to be out in it yet, especially on my own. It's dead easy to drive.'

'So it might be, but you don't want to get nicked,' cautioned Ben.

The lad-chat went on and by the time Jamie left, Ben felt a whole lot happier and felt more inclined to begin what he knew would have to be done sooner or later; sorting out his dad's stuff.

That night in his own bed he slept better than he had since 'that' day. He managed to get himself into a position with his arm which wasn't too uncomfortable and had a good eight hours. The following morning having discovered nothing in the pantry to eat for breakfast he walked round to his grandparents' hoping he might get a fry-up. His luck was in. Mabel, making a fuss of him as usual sat him down at the kitchen table and served up a sausage, two rashers of bacon, a fried egg, bread and marge and a cup of tea.

'He'll be spoiled,' muttered his grandad.

'I'd help you with the washing up grandma but it's a bit tricky with, well, you know, my arm.'

'I suppose I'll have to let you off this time then?' chuckled Mabel.

'Don't you get thinking you can get away with that excuse for long,' piped up his Grandad.

After breakfast was all cleared away and at Albert's suggestion the three of them caught the bus into town to see the funeral director.

'I thought we'd use the Co-op,' said Albert. 'They give a good service so I'm told besides which your Gran can get the divvy then as well.'

The preliminary arrangements were made with the funeral director who undertook to collect the body from the coroner's mortuary. For their part the family would fix a date for the funeral with the vicar at St Catherine's, put an obituary notice in the local paper and inform all those who needed to know.

'Who's going to pay for the funeral and everything?' asked Ben.

'I suppose that'll be me' stated Albert. 'I've got some savings don't worry. I know he was your dad but he was my son!'

'I guess I'll have to leave school and get a job now,' suggested Ben.

'You'll do no such bloody thing,' insisted his grandad. 'You'll be going into the sixth form in September and off to college in a couple of years. Your dad, me and your gran, never had the chance. You're certainly not going to waste your opportunity. We've got high hopes of you making something of yourself.' The tone of grandad's delivery left absolutely no doubt in Ben's mind that his immediate future was assured.

'But I'll need...'

'You're my responsibility now. We'll look after you. I've got some War Bonds I can cash in if it comes to it. That should cover some if not all the expense. Your dad must have some stuff we can sell as well. So there's an end to it and no argument!' Albert had no idea just how prophetic his final statement would prove to be.

Ben felt that an enormous burden had been lifted from his shoulders. He would be staying at school studying A-levels in music, English literature and history. He could continue to see Tina and possibly most importantly, his determination to get back onto a piano stool was redoubled.

Chapter Thirty-Five

During the next few days Ben had a great deal to do. He went to the Registrar's office. The coroner had already been in touch with the Registrar and Ben was given the death certificate and a certificate for burial to pass on to the undertaker. Ben was no longer phased by any of this. Ok, Ken was his dad but the relationship over the years had become strained to say the least. They were just not getting on, no question. What's more it was a great relief to Ben to know that he would not have to put up with any more physical, verbal or mental abuse. He knew that he would be far better off with his grandparents; that his prospects would be altogether improved beyond measure. Albert and Mabel had agreed that Ben should move in to live with them. They had room and Mabel wouldn't have to worry about whether or not he was getting fed properly and taking care of himself. There was also the bonus of there being a piano in the spare room upon which he could practise. Ben felt entirely liberated; that his life was almost starting again from square one.

Ben went to the council offices to let them know he would no longer want the house. He handed over his father's rent book. In return for giving up the lease on the house, he was told that there would be a partial refund of rent. He was requested to move out as soon as possible. To qualify for the refund, he only had until the end of the week to vacate the house so the pressure was on. Jamie and Diane and Tina were only too happy to help out. And when it actually came to it there wasn't a great deal of stuff anyway. Just a few sticks of utility furniture, clothes and that was about it. Ben couldn't imagine what his grandad had been referring to amongst his dad's stuff that might be saleable.

The day of the funeral came. It was a sombre occasion but the only tears that were shed were Mabel's. The Reverend Pugh delivered a short service and gave a eulogy which Ben thought he'd probably composed for someone else. Old Pugh was extolling the virtues of someone and the description he was giving didn't sound like his dad at all. The small group of mourners then gathered at the graveside. Albert and Mabel, Ben, his uncle Keith and aunty Joyce, Ken's siblings and a small dapper bloke wearing a bus driver's uniform who Ben didn't know. There was also a woman he didn't recognise. She spoke briefly to Mabel after the service then smiled at Ben and disappeared. Afterwards it was back to what was now Ben's family home. Mabel had prepared a few sandwiches and there was tea or a bottle of Everards'. And that was that.

'Who was that woman you spoke to at the funeral?' Ben later asked his grandma. Mabel gave Albert an anxious glance. She was obviously unsure of whether she should be honest or not.

'That was Helen, your mother.'

There was silence for a moment. His grandparents didn't quite know what sort of reaction to expect and were quite startled when it came.

'Why didn't you tell me, why was I not introduced, why was I not told?' Ben exploded with incredulity. He got up from the table and stormed out of the kitchen and up the stairs to his room.

'It had to happen sooner or later,' said Albert sagely. 'He has a right to know.'

Ben didn't appear for lunch and it was with some relief that later in the day Albert and Mabel heard the piano; the sound of scales in the lower octaves. Ben was giving the fingers of his left hand a workout. It had been some time. After a while he very sheepishly came into the kitchen where Mabel was peeling potatoes.

'Sorry Grandma,' apologised Ben. 'I shouldn't have gone off like that.'

The apology was accepted and after tea, he was consoled further as Albert related some of the background to his parents' breakup.

'It wasn't long after the war. Your dad hadn't been back long before he and your mam were married. It wasn't long after that that she was carrying you. That's when it all started to go pear-shaped.' Mabel took up the narrative.

'Not that we'll ever know the reason why now but he changed. Maybe it was the fatigue of war, the lack of money, the rationing, the uncertainty of the future, a responsibility he wasn't prepared for, goodness knows how many reasons.'

Albert interrupted.

'Or something more sinister such as the bloody black market or trouble with the police.'

Ben found it hard to contain his surprise at his grandad's accusatory tone. His grandad continued.

'It was about the time when the Yanks dropped them atom bombs on the Japs. I reckon something had happened, something about as explosive as those bombs. He wouldn't have upped and left just like that, not with your mam in the family way, no not our Ken.' There was a sadness, a tenderness in his voice. They both looked at Ben. There was compassion and sympathy in their eyes.

'At the funeral' Mabel continued, 'your mam asked me

if it would be ok if she could pay a visit, try to get to know you and make up for all those lost years. I told her it was not for me to say but that we'd put her request to you when the time was right.' Ben was about to speak but before he could get his words out. Albert, reverting to his normal assertive self said, 'Anyway, don't decide here and now. Sleep on it, give it some thought. You're under no pressure either way. And whatever you decide, me and your gran'll be behind you."

His grandad's reassurance was comforting in a way but did little to ease the anxiety he was now feeling. What would he say to her? What would she say to him? What would she expect? What did he expect? There were unknown quantities in abundance and just when he thought his life was back on track and he had the route map for the long, straight road to his future. He resolved to get an opinion from Tina.

Chapter Thirty-Six

It was the beginning of September. Just another week before they were back to school as sixth formers. Ben and Tina were sitting on a bench midway between their two villages, each having walked halfway. Ben explained how a 'mystery woman' had turned up to his dad's funeral. Tina listened intently. Sparing no details at all Ben gave a full account of his dad leaving before he had been born and how the mystery woman had turned out to be his mother; the mother who had all but abandoned him and had 'buggered off' to quote his dad. He asked what Tina thought about him letting his mother back into his life.

Tina sat and thought about it for quite some time before making any comment at all and when she finally did, it wasn't particularly helpful.

"What does your gran think?"

"Neither Gran nor Grandad have really expressed an opinion either way. They've suggested I 'think about it' as it has to be my decision in the end."

'And have you?'

'Have I what?'

'Thought about it.'

'Apart from thinking about you, I've thought of nothing else.

They were watching the combine harvester in the field opposite where they sat. Tina switched on the small transistor radio she'd brought with her. The Percy Faith Orchestra was playing 'Theme from a Summer Place'. She thought of this tune as their accompanying theme for the holiday which sadly was about to end. Tina switched off the radio, midway through the 'Summer' Place' and in such a demonstrative way to signify she had something to say.

'I think you should get your gran to invite your mum round for a cup of tea. You'll have a much better idea of whether you want your mum in your life when you've had a chance to talk to her.'

'Ok,' said Ben, 'that's what I'll do.'

After sitting and chatting about school, the sixth form and what they were both intending to do, and with a kiss and cuddle every now and then, Tina walked back with Ben. They stopped at the first phone kiosk and Tina called her dad and asked him to come and pick her up. When he got home, Ben told his Gran what had been decided. Mabel agreed it was probably the best way ahead and suggested that she would try and arrange such a meeting for one afternoon when he had no school or other commitments.

The following day Ben was due at the hospital. Since the accident and his subsequent discharge from hospital Ben's hand, as far as he could tell, was mending. There were periods of pins and needles which he had been told to expect as a good sign and various other sensations which Ben took as an indication that his hand was getting better. Dennis, Tina's dad, had agreed to take Ben into Leicester for his appointment at the infirmary. He needed to get some supplies from the Southgate Street Brewery anyway. Ben, with Tina's help eventually found his way to the appropriate outpatients' clinic and registered with the receptionist. They took seats in the waiting room. Tina idly flicked through a very old edition of *Harper's* magazine. They whispered to each other whenever there was anything happening which was worthwhile commenting on. It wasn't too long before a nurse appeared from a side room. She had a file under her arm, took a look at it and called Ben's name. 'Irish, by the sound of her,' thought Ben.

Leaving Tina in the waiting room with a fairly bountiful supply of old magazines, Ben followed the nurse into a treatment room. A technician sat with a pair of shears which looked like a hybrid of scissors, tin-snips and garden shears. Within a few moments, the plaster was off. Resisting the instant reaction to scratch his arm, Ben attempted to move his fingers but the nurse gave him a look that said 'Don't'.

'Please be keeping your hand perfectly still now,' she ordered. 'We'll be needing to take an X-ray first, and then Mr Courtenay will be wanting to see you.'

With the nurse leading the way off they went to the radiology department. After a short wait the radiologist had taken three x-rays, and Ben was herded back to the original waiting room. Tina had moved to a different seat. Ben went a sat beside her. Together they examined his hand. It had all but reverted to a normal size but his fingers were still slightly swollen. There was very little evidence of the bruising, but the skin looked tight around the scar tissue across his palm and the areas around the ends of the wires which had been inserted to pin the bones together looked sore.

This cursory self-examination was interrupted by the nurse who asked him to return to the treatment room.

'Hello again Bob,' said Mr Courtenay.

'It's Ben sir,' corrected Ben

'Yes of course.' 'If he can't get my name right what chance have my fingers got?' thought Ben.

Mr Courtenay and the nurse were intently studying the x-ray pictures.

'Good. In fact very good!' Mr Courtenay exclaimed. 'Yes, the proximal phalanges and metacarpals have knitted nicely. You're a very lucky young man. I think we can safely remove the pins now, nurse.'

The look of horror on Ben's face prompted the nurse to reassure him that he wouldn't feel a thing.

'Now don't you get worrying there, you'll be having a local anaesthetic.' No sooner said, she produced a syringe and inserted the needle into the fleshy part of Ben's hand just above the wrist. Within moments Ben's hand was numb. With a small pair of what looked like pliers, Mr Courtenay skilfully removed the pins which he placed in a stainless steel dish on the table.

'There. All done.'

'Thank you, sir.'

'You're welcome Bob!' and off he disappeared.

The nurse then explained that another plaster cast would be required, but only for a couple of weeks, after which intensive rehabilitation sessions with a specialist hand therapist would soon have him playing the piano again.

'How did you know I played the piano?' Ben was curious.

'Well now, it's in your notes so it is!'

They both laughed at the unintentional pun.

Chapter Thirty-Seven

Ben returned to hospital accompanied by Tina thanks to Dennis who had given them a lift. It was the day for the removal of the second plaster cast and he was nervous, not about the removal process, there was nothing to that, but about the state his hand would be in when the plaster came off. He checked into the outpatients' clinic and he and Tina sat in the waiting room. Dennis had gone to the bank to pay in the previous weekend's takings.

Tina had a look through the pile of magazines and apart from those in which she had no interest she'd read them all and even though the last time she had kept Ben company at the clinic had been almost three weeks ago there were no new ones. A familiar voice broke the silence; the Irish nurse. She and Ben exchanged pleasantries and he was ushered into the room where the technician sat with his shears. A few snips later and the plaster was off.

'That looks absolutely fine, to be sure, so it does. How does it feel?'

Ben, looked at his hand as if seeing it for the first time. It looked ok. Tentatively he attempted to move his fingers.

'You'll not be getting much movement just yet,' the nurse informed him. 'Does it feel ok, is there any pain?'

'It feels fine and there's no pain as such,' Ben answered.

The disappointment in the tone of his voice was all too apparent.

'Well that's good then. I'm now to take you to the physiotherapy department. We'd better take your young lady with us or one or the other of you will get lost.' The nurse stuck her head around the door to the waiting room and beckoned over towards Tina. Whilst they were walking down the corridor the nurse explained what the next steps in his rehabilitation were.

'I'm not sure who you'll be seeing, but he, or she will be responsible for your therapy and you'll be given exercises to do. You be making sure you do them too.' She turned to Tina, 'You'll see that he does now.' It was an instruction not a request.

'Do I have to see Mr Courtenay again?' Ben asked.

'Oh, no. That's a good sign. When the surgeon no longer wants to see you, that means he's happy with the work he's done. Almost a guarantee, don't you know, to be sure it is.'

They arrived at the physiotherapy department. The Irish nurse checked with the receptionist who sat behind a desk in an area that to Ben's eye looked to be somewhere between a treatment room and a gymnasium.

'You'll be seeing Dorothy. She'll be responsible for your treatment.'

'Will I be seeing you again?' Ben asked. He'd taken a bit of a shine to the Irish nurse.

'Oh yes, to be sure you will. I'll be on the front row of your concert at the De Montfort Hall,' she joked.

'Thanks for everything,' Ben called after her as she left.

Tina was just a little bit concerned that Dorothy might be someone she would be jealous of; a challenger for Ben's affections. It was a commonly held misconception that male patients fell for the nurses that treated them. In the event Tina's worries were instantly dispelled upon the appearance of Dorothy.

'Hello, Ben?' she enquired. 'I'm Dorothy. You can call me Dot.'

Ben cast his gaze upon this formidable looking woman who was built like an all-in heavyweight wrestler.

Tina took a seat in the waiting area and was relieved to find some fresh reading material although watching the various activities going on in the department was far more entertaining than any magazine. Dot had herded Ben just a short distance away and was examining his hand. Tina couldn't quite hear what was being said but she could see that there was some manner of manipulation going on. After an hour Ben's initial therapy session was at an end. He was given an appointment card with a schedule of dates upon which he should present himself for further treatment sessions. He also had a sheet of paper with schematic diagrams and descriptions of the exercises he was to do on a daily basis.

Sitting in the back of Dennis' car Ben explained to Tina what Dot had said and he tried to demonstrate some of the exercises. Dennis was taking an interest and suggested that although he knew nothing about such matters he imagined that exercises on the piano would be as good as any physiotherapy. Looking at his therapy sheet Ben was thinking Dennis might have a point.

The first day of the autumn term came. Mabel roused Ben early and made sure he had a proper breakfast. Since he'd moved in with his grandparents, Mabel had been to the haberdashery on one of her visits to town and bought the red braid which she'd then sewn around the edges of Ben's blazer. Sixth-formers were identified by this distinction. Apart from that there hadn't been any major expense with regard to his school uniform although she had noticed that the collars on a couple of shirts needed turning.

Ben's grandparents stood proudly on their front doorstep

and watched him leave. As he cycled off Albert was pleased to see that his advice about wearing a glove on the right hand had been taken. Ben had been put into a form with other students specialising in 'arts' subjects, as distinct from sciences. His form tutor, who coincidentally would also be his English teacher was Mr Howkins. Ben was happy on two counts. Mr Howkins was not only a great character, but a superb pianist. Ben had heard him accompany the review which the Upper Sixth always presented before they left school for good. His 'stride' technique was masterful and tremendously impressive. It was a style which Ben hoped he would be good enough to emulate one day. Secondly, as Tina was also studying arts subjects, she too was in the same form.

Up until the end of the fifth form Ben had been playing the piano for assembly. The Headmaster, Mr Oldham's, secretary would come along at registration with details of the hymn to be sung, and with just the occasional exception Ben could churn out the hymn tune from sight. As Mr Howkins was completing the register Mr Oldham's secretary appeared. After locating Ben in the room, she handed a slip of paper to Ben. The hymn was to be 'The School Song' – 'Set in Proud England's Heart'; traditional on the first day of the new school year. Ben was crestfallen. Before he could explain his situation to the secretary she'd gone. Having witnessed what had happened Mr Howkins came over to Ben's desk where Tina was attempting to console him, discreetly, of course.

'Don't worry Ben. Mr Oldham clearly hasn't been apprised of your non-availability for the time being, nor the reasons for it.' Ben drew a long breath of relief.

'I'll be your deputy this morning and for the time being. Maybe Mr Sims can take a turn now and again as well. I'll explain the cause of your 'indisposition' to Mr Oldham.

He's bound to understand and it's unlikely you'll fall out of his favour as a result.'

'Thanks, sir,' said Ben. 'It hadn't occurred to me that school wouldn't have been informed. Have you got my change of address as well?'

Assembly went without a hitch, although Ben's presence in the ranks rather than on the platform drew a few quizzical looks. By the end of the day it seemed that everyone was aware of what had happened. Members of staff and students alike were approaching him offering sympathy, condolences and good wishes for an expeditious recovery.

In English, the class was introduced to *King Lear* which would be one the set texts for A-level. In History, the very elderly Miss Mountford's dissertation on the repeal of the Corn Laws was hardly riveting. In fact Ben wondered if she'd not done the repealing personally. She looked old enough. Then there'd been a 'free' period when Ben and Tina had sat in the sanctity of the library, whilst others had preferred the sixth form common room The last session of the day had been a music lesson in which Mr Sims sought to introduce his charges to the wonder of cadential and passing second inversion chords. Homework was the harmonisation of a Bach Chorale. And that was it. Day one as a sixth-former was over. He gave Tina a quick kiss as she got on the school bus to Sapcote then collected his bike from the racks hoping that Grandma had got something good for tea.

Chapter Thirty-Eight

It was October half-term holiday. Ben was practising the piano. The dexterity in his right hand was gradually returning. His physiotherapy sessions with Dot were beginning to prove their value although it really was very tedious getting to Leicester and back on Midland Red once a week.

'You just be grateful for the National Health Service and all this free treatment you're getting. You wouldn't have been so lucky ten years ago!' Mabel was always extolling the virtues of the NHS and quite rightly so. Still for Ben, once a week to Leicester for a torture session with 'Olga the Ogre' as he had nicknamed Dot, his physiotherapist, was a chore.

Of far greater benefit to his way of thinking was the copy of *The Physiological Mechanics of Piano Technique* lent to him by Mr Sims. He was really getting stuck into that. Also giving his fingers a daily workout were one or more of *Fifty-One Exercises* by Brahms. Subtitled *Melodic Finger Exercises for use in preparation for the performance of his challenging Piano Works*, the exercises were proving to be challenging enough. Occasionally from the spare room came the sound of the piano lid being slammed shut when the exercises were making demands on the pianist that he was struggling to meet! However, his piano playing was improving in leaps and bounds.

Mabel answered the front door.

'Hello Helen, it's been a long time. Please, come in.'
Helen stepped into the hallway. She had clearly made a great
effort with her appearance. With her blonde hair tied back
and wearing a very expensive looking suit she looked very
sophisticated. She turned her head towards the spare room.

'Goodness, who is that playing the piano?' she enquired.

'That,' exclaimed Mabel gushing with pride, 'is your son!'

'I don't believe it.' Helen was quite incredulous.

Mabel called to her grandson,

'Ben there's someone here to see you.'

The three of them went into the living room where Albert
was already sitting. He stood as they entered and moved
to shake Helen's hand but hesitated and with a change of
mind, gave her a hug.

'I'm really pleased you've come back to us.' Mabel went
to the kitchen and made a pot of tea which she brought
through to the living room on a tray with the best china.
Albert had resumed his armchair.

'Hello Ben.' Helen was fighting back tears of joy. 'We
have met before but that would have been seventeen years
ago when I was only three years older than you are now.'

Ben offered his hand which still bore the scars of his accident quite visibly.

'Hello mother.' His manners were impeccable. 'Won't
you sit down please?'

'Am I allowed to give my son a hug?' Helen asked, but
didn't wait for an answer. Mother and son embraced after
which Helen sat to attention in the other armchair. Ben sat
beside his grandmother on the sofa.

Mabel poured the tea and there was something of an
embarrassing silence between them all. It was Helen who
broke the ice.

'I expect you're all wondering where I've been; why I left
and didn't get in touch.'

She continued with a reasonably detailed synopsis of her part in the previous seventeen years. Mabel and Albert both had many questions and Albert didn't hold back with his disapproval of some of Helen's answers. Ben sat in silence alternately staring at his mother and then to one or other of his grandparents.

The inquisition continued and the matter of Ken's death was raised. Neither Albert, Mabel nor Ben were aware that Helen had witnessed it. Albert retrieved the coroner's report from where it was still filed behind the clock on the mantelpiece. He handed it to Helen, who was now crying quite openly. She read it, her tears dropping onto the paper. Ben handed her a tissue from a box on the sideboard and sat on the arm of the chair with his arm around her shoulders.

'I think he must have hit his head as he fell from the boat; maybe on the wall of the lock.' This was the only untruth she told.

After almost an hour-and-a-half Helen's past history had been revealed, questions answered honestly and frankly, explanations given. Silence prevailed once more. This time it was Mabel who interrupted the stillness.

'There's a plate of sandwiches and some fancy cakes in the kitchen. Be a love and fetch them please Ben.' Ben did as he was bidden and returned carrying the tray.

'So, where are you staying?' enquired Albert.

'With Rosemary, you know Rosemary my sister. It's a bit cramped but it won't be for long. I know it's money that has not been honestly made, but I intend to buy a small house somewhere fairly locally. I hope you won't mind.' Helen could see by his body language that Albert had a very low opinion of the money being spent in such a way. She attempted to redress his disquiet.

'What's left after all the expenses, I'll put in trust for Ben.' This went some way towards meeting with Albert's approval. Helen continued, 'I've got an appointment to view a cottage just outside Great Glen tomorrow. If it's suitable, and if…" she paused, swallowed and took a deep breath, '… and if he would like to I'd love it if Ben were to move in with me.' Ben and his grandparents looked askance at each other.

'If you approve, of course,' she hastily added.

'That'll need some careful consideration,' Albert said. 'There's his school and his piano practice, oh yes, and his girlfriend of course. But it'll be for Ben to decide, not us. You're his mother and it's only right, but we'll be very sad to see him leave us.'

With that there wasn't much more to say. Ben would take a look at the cottage his mother intended to buy and make a decision after some very careful thought about the logistics and implications and after talking to Tina, obviously.

Chapter Thirty-Nine

Helen left her meeting with her son and parents-in-law feeling quite uplifted. She was reminded of a passage from a book she had read once upon a time somewhere, or had she heard it from a pulpit perhaps on one of the few occasions she'd been to church?

When you perform any task, it is easier than it seems in anticipation or even in retrospect because the different problems offer themselves little by little and in simplified form until no major and complex problem remains.

'Never did this sage reflection seem more appropriate than right now,' thought Helen. And with that in mind, she felt confident about calling in on Frank. She was glad she'd decided against the high heels option when getting dressed earlier because it was quite a distance to Waring's Farm. Even so her choice of footwear was hardly comfortable for a long walk.

It was almost dark when she arrived and walking up the lane it seemed like only a few days ago that she last did it. In fact she half-expected to see Frank sucking on his pipe and tinkering with his tractor when she arrived in the farmyard. But where was the old Massey Harris? And what was this? A brand-new John Deere by the look of it. With slight trepidation but buoyed up by the way the family encounter had gone Helen knocked on the farmhouse door. She could hear *The Archers* signature tune from inside the kitchen. Frank opened the door.

'Is it…? It bloody well is! 'elen! Well, I never did! Bugger me, here's a ghost from me past!'

'Hello Frank.'

'Yo' got a hug for an ol' farmer – I might stink a bit,' he cautioned.

Helen eagerly walked into his open arms and held him tightly. *It is easier than it seems in anticipation...* She accepted his invitation – more of an order really – to join him for supper.

'T'ain't much, I'll admit, but a bowl o' my stew and dumplin's'll stick to yo' ribs.'

They ate, occasionally smiling at each other from opposite ends of the table.

'Now then my gal, I ain't a-goin' to pry. Yo'll tell me if yo' want me know. I'm just so 'appy that yo've come back. I know Ernie'll be pleased as well. And Kate and her Stuart, she got wed yo' know. They were sad when you left like that.' Frank rattled and prattled on.

'I' got a bottle o' Everards 'ere in the pantry – we should celebrate.' He fetched the beer and split the bottle between two glasses.

' 'eres to my 'elen. Cheers love an' welcome 'ome.' They drank and Frank lit his pipe.

'Please may I beg a favour Frank?'

'Name it!'

'Would you give me a lift to my sister's please? These shoes are killing me.'

'I thought it were goin' to be summat serious,' he joked.

'Oh well, in that case, can I carry on with my driving lessons?'

After sitting and chatting for an hour, Helen decided it was time to go. Frank got his old tweed jacket and tossed the car keys onto the table.

''Ere yo' go then, better start now.'

They went into the barn, Helen looked round for the Austin.

'Frank! You've got a new car! A Jaguar!'

'A beauty ain't she. Mark 9 Jaguar! The Austin did me proud but she died. Bit like ol' Massey 'arris. He' a gonna an' all.'

Helen hadn't lost her touch, despite not having driven for such a long time. The Jaguar was automatic and so much easier to handle than the Austin had been. On the drive to Rosemary's house she told Frank about her black marketeering as he'd known about its beginnings anyway. She also told him about her ill-gotten fortune and her intention to buy a house and have Ben move in with her. Frank approved wholeheartedly.

The following day, having given his 'lad' a list of jobs for the day, Frank picked Helen up from Rosemary's house and Helen then drove over to Burton Overy, the village near Great Glen. With a small population of around 300 it sounded like Utopia and Helen had arranged to meet the estate agent and view the cottage. When they arrived the agent was standing beside the white-painted wicket fence which separated the narrow lane from the front garden of the cottage. Frank lit his pipe and stood, hands on hips looking at the property and nodding wisely. Helen knew the moment she saw it that this would become her home. It was a real 'chocolate box' cottage; pretty enough to feature as a jigsaw puzzle picture. It even had a large shed around the back which would serve as a garage for the car she intended to buy.

During the tour of inspection which was accompanied by 'agentspeak' to which she paid no attention whatsoever, Helen was much too busy deciding which would be her bedroom, which would be Ben's? Is this room big enough for a piano? Oh look! An inglenook fireplace! The cottage was everything she'd had imagined and more. It was everything she wanted and then some!

They stood outside the half-timbered cottage; 'Marsh Cottage'. The sloping meadow land leading down to the River Sence, where the cottage stood, still had a wild beauty about it with tall grasses in their autumnal glory in which daisies, vetch, poppies and gorse still flowered. Helen was transfixed by it all and she informed the agent that 'without a doubt' she was going to buy the property and it should be removed from the market immediately. She would call at the agency office tomorrow and complete the formalities; pay a deposit or the whole amount if required, she was so keen. She would instruct a solicitor and do whatever else was necessary. And she did just as she had assured the agent she would.

Frank was too busy on the farm to take Helen to Leicester the next day, so she was obliged to travel by Midland Red. The journey brought back certain memories she would rather not have had. Anyway after her visit to the estate agency she had three more calls to make. The first was to the driving test centre to book an appointment for her test. The second, to an Austin franchise dealership where she ordered a brand-new Austin Mini, a white one, for which she paid £629 cash, there and then. She left the salesman with the instruction that she would collect it in three weeks' time after her driving test, such was her confidence! Helen's third call was to Wright's Musical Instrument Shop in Upper Conduit Street, off London Road, quite near the railway station. She enquired about buying a piano.

'I want the best available for my son. He's to become a concert pianist you know.'

The salesman gave the impression that he had heard it all before from parents with delusions of greatness for their offspring.

'If I might make so bold you'll be needing a Steinway then madam." 'Who is this fellow, pretentious twerp? Bet he can't play as well as my Ben,' Helen thought.

'We can order one for you if you'd so care? They come from Germany you know so it'll take maybe a month to arrive. Would madam care to leave a 10% deposit?"

Helen delved once more into her handbag and, with a look, she handed over £125. The salesman took a pace backwards in astonishment.

On leaving the shop she pondered.

'If 10% is £125, the full price is...' Somewhat taken aback she drew on Frank's vocabulary.

'Bugger me, more than the bloody car!'

Chapter Forty

Ben went to visit his mother at Aunty Rosemary's on several occasions. There was a great deal of catching up to done and often they would stroll around Hollycroft Park doing exactly that, catching up. Helen took a lot of photographs with the camera she intended to give to her brother Sid, but she hadn't got around to making the presentation yet. She wanted to know all about Ben's formative years from his earliest memories through to being dumped, and she actually used the word 'dumped' on his grandparents. Could he remember anything of his 'uncles', Ernie and Frank? What about Aunty Kate, did he remember her? How did he enjoy keeping chickens in his grandparents' garden? How did he feel when he eventually moved into the new council house with his dad? And the piano playing! When had he decided he wanted to learn to play the piano? There was one topic of questioning that Helen returned to many times. Ken, re-joining the army. Had Ben's grandparents ever referred to what the reasons may have been? Did Ken ever get any mail or receive any visitors? What was he really up to? Was he actually in Scotland?

So many questions but not many answers especially to those which involved his dad. It was as if Helen knew her husband was up to something and not of the adulterous affair variety either. Ken may have been many things but never a womaniser. He would not have left all that black market loot behind knowing its value and the profit which would be realised. What on earth had been going on?

Ben told his mum all about passing the 11-plus exam and going to the grammar school; how his dad had bought him a new bike; his piano lessons; trainspotting with his mate Jamie. Ultimately he described how on 'that' day, a day that should have been a special day out with his girlfriend, he discovered his dad's body in the canal lock and the accident to his hand. He relived the pain of the surgery and the physiotherapy sessions with Olga the Ogre. Ben admitted that the memory of the sight of his dad's body floating face down still sometimes gave him nightmares. Helen knew nothing of any of this of course but she listened intently, sympathetically and with all manner of maternal feelings she never knew she had, not having experienced such love and affection until now.

Helen's property purchase was going ahead with contracts having been exchanged. It was just a matter of time now before the sale was completed and she could move in. One day when they were out together it had come on to rain and they took shelter in the Ardern Café. Over coffee Helen did her best in a very subtle way to persuade Ben that he should move in with her. She showed him the estate agent's particulars and painted a very idyllic scene which she hoped would appeal. Helen was ultra-careful not to come over as pushy or put him off by being over-persuasive. Ben had lots of questions. Could he have a television set in his bedroom? Could he keep chickens? How would he get to school? Could Tina come and visit. Helen did her very best to convince him that no problem or difficulty would be insurmountable, and he could have pretty much anything he wanted. Such was Helen's desire; her need to make up for lost time. She wasn't looking for Ben's sympathy but explained that having now caught up with her son, he had helped to ease her conscience-stricken regret. Helen left Ben in no doubt as to her sincerity. Her remorse knew no bounds.

Helen was absolutely thrilled when Ben announced that he wanted to visit the cottage and take a look. Could he bring Tina? She must meet Tina!

When Ben initially broke the news to Tina that he might be moving to live in Burton Overy, her reaction was one of great sadness.

'That means we'll only ever get to see each other at school.' To say she was not amused would be understating her disapproval. Ben attempted to reason with her.

'Look Tina, it's really not much further away than we are at the moment. One of us has to beg a lift or catch a bus, or we both bike and meet in the middle. I'd be as sad as you if we only ever saw each other at school.' Tina took consolation from Ben's reasoning.

'Look, I've suggested to mum that we both go and have a look at her new cottage. She's already said that you can come and visit whenever you like. Perhaps even stay over if you like.'

After school that day Tina didn't bother with the school bus. She and Ben walked hand in hand to the town library. They both had some studying to do and besides it was a good excuse for them to spend time in each other's company. When the library closed they walked back to his grandparents' house for tea. He knew his grandma wouldn't mind. Tina could then get her dad to come and collect her, she hoped!

It was the afternoon before the driving test and Helen had gone to see Frank for a final lesson. She'd promised to prepare and cook his favourite tea in return provided he would take her to the driving test centre and let her borrow the Jaguar for the actual test.

'Yo' know yo' can wrap me round yo' little finger,' conceded Frank. He collected Helen from Rosemary's house around lunchtime the next day. She slid into the driving seat.

'Now don't forget – mirror, signal, manoeuvre,' he instructed, and off they went.

Frank spent a nervous forty minutes in the test centre waiting room, much to the annoyance of one candidate waiting for her appointment. His pipe was emitting a real pungent smog! When Helen returned, wreathed in smiles, she stood in the middle of the room and ripped her 'L' plates into small pieces and threw them into the air like confetti.

'I'm a-guessin' yo' passed then?' Frank jested.

'Would you now take me to Evans' please?'

'Evans'? What, yo' mean the car showroom place?'

'Yes please, you know where it is?'

'Of course!' Although he didn't understand why she wanted to go there.

Frank pulled onto the forecourt and parked. Helen skipped into the showroom. Her car was ready. The salesman handed her a cardboard folder containing her guarantee, owner's manual, the service-book and logbook (made out with the new address) and her insurance certificate.

'Would you like me to show you the controls, miss?' Helen declined the salesman's offer.

'Thanks, but I think I'll manage.' She was oozing confidence.

Helen thanked Frank for waiting, then explained that he needn't have bothered. Now he understood!

Chapter Forty-One

Helen drove directly to the grammar school and parked close to the layby where the school buses waited. It was almost 4 pm. She knew Ben would walk Tina to the bus and she couldn't wait to see his face – his mum in a brand new Mini! She'd get to meet Tina as well.

The wait wasn't long! There was Ben pushing his bike and presumably the extremely attractive young woman who was hand in hand with him was Tina. She stepped out of the car but neither Ben nor Tina saw her.

'Had a good day you two?' she enquired.

'Mum!' Ben's jaw dropped. 'What're you doing here?'

'Aren't you going to introduce me?' Then remembering his manners, 'Sorry! Mum this Tina, Christina Mason. Tina this is my mum, Helen Blake.'

Each was pleased to meet the other.

'And this,' drooled Helen, 'is my new car!'

Both Tina and Ben were lost for all but one word.

'Wow!' they uttered in unison.

Helen got in the car, started the engine, then, mirror, signal, manoeuvre, pulled out and sped off leaving her son and his girlfriend staring after her, open-mouthed but speechless.

It was the weekend. After completing two hours piano

practice and cleaning out the chicken shed, Ben excused himself.

'I'm going to see Tina, if that's ok?'

'Of course, lad. Mind how you go. Shall I do you some tea?'

'I don't know what time I'll be back Grandma. Don't worry about me, I'll get some chips.'

And off he went. He hadn't been gone more than ten minutes when there was a knock at the front door. Mabel opened the door.

'Helen, what a surprise.'

'Hello Mabel. I really came to see Ben, see if he'd like a ride in my new car,' she said indicating the car gleaming white in the autumn sunshine. Mabel explained that she had just missed him but she'd catch up with him at the Red Lion in Sapcote where Tina lived. If they weren't there, Dennis, Tina's dad would surely know.

Sure enough Helen passed Ben on the road even before he'd got to Sapcote She gave him a wave and tooted as she overtook. The Mini was parked outside the Red Lion when Ben arrived a few minutes later.

'I don't know what you two have got planned, but I thought we could all go over to Burton and I could show you around the new cottage.'

Ben went around the back of the pub to the living quarters and knocked on the door. He was obviously expected. Tina answered the door herself and Ben, slightly embarrassed, explained that his mum wanted to show off the new house to them both – probably show off her new car as well. Tina's response took Ben by surprise.

'That'd be nice. I think I'll like your mum. Young isn't she?'

They all piled into the Mini and the drive to Burton took about thirty minutes. Tina had expected it to take longer.

The front garden was a picture in the sunshine. Roses, chrysanthemums and dahlias in a variety of colours radiant against the freshly whitewashed, pebble-dashed walls of the cottage.

'It's gorgeous, what a beautiful little house, I'd love to live here instead of in a smelly pub.'

'You can,' responded Helen, 'just whenever you like.' Ben was blushing.

'I am now the very proud owner although I can't move in until next week. The decorators have not quite finished inside yet. Welcome to Marsh Cottage!' Tina and Ben followed Helen inside for the guided tour of the accommodation. A living room-cum-kitchen with a separate pantry and back door to the garden, a sitting-room with ingle-nook fireplace, a dining room and upstairs three-bedrooms and a box-room that had been converted into a bathroom.

'Oh, Mrs Blake, it's the prettiest house I ever seen.'

'Please, call me Helen.'

And that was enough to clinch the arrangement. Ben would move from his grandparents' and live with his mum. And then just in case any other incentive were needed Helen added,

'To make the travelling a little easier Ben, I'll get you a car for your eighteenth birthday.' The extra incentive was superfluous but very welcome all the same. 'Jamie, eat your heart out!' thought Ben.

They all took a walk around the village and a leisurely drive back to the Red Lion. The pub was just opening, and Helen was introduced to Tina's folks. There were no other customers as yet so they all sat in the snug and drank shandy. Eventually Helen left and Tina's mum produced a plate of sausage and mash for the young couple.

Chapter Forty-Two

To the casual observer the group of men gathered around Lock Number 25, The Top Half-Mile Lock at Newton Harcourt, may have been the members of the local angling club organising a fishing competition. However they were in fact carrying out a preliminary investigation into a complaint about the operation of the lock. The flow of water through one of the paddles on the lower gates was impeded and thus slowing down the rate at which the lock would empty. They filled and emptied the lock several times and confirmed the veracity of the complaint. They went away.

'I wonder what that was all about?' Jamie was talking to Diane as they sat watching from the warmth of the Triumph Herald parked on the Wain Bridge. It was almost eighteen months since Jamie and Diane had got together. They now seemed to be 'an item' and, as when they were younger, this area around Newton Harcourt was still a favourite spot. It was tranquil, peaceful with little risk of being disturbed or observed. Another thing the locality had going for it, from their perspective, was the fact that, just up the road at Great Glen, they could get served in the Old Greyhound with no questions asked and unlikely to be found out.

Two days later a van arrived at lock Number 25. *British Waterways Board* said the sign writing on the panels of the van. Two men in orange overalls and lifejackets got out of the van. One of them took a telescopic pole from the rear of the van. The other man was winding up the fully operational paddle and the lock was slowly emptying. The pole man had extended it and was probing the depths by the blocked paddle.

'I reckon there's summat blocking the paddle, Ted,' pole man said to his mate.

'Yeah, I can definitely feel summat.' Ted walked across the gates and relieved pole man of his pole so that he could have a prod himself.

'You're right Dick!" Ted dropped the open paddle, Dick retracted the pole and replaced it in the van. They stood and weighed up the situation whilst they had a smoke. Eventually they came to the conclusion that a small boat would be required from where whatever the offending blockage was, it might be grappled with a hook and from there hauled out of the water. They went away.

Jamie and Diane were becoming regular customers at the Old Greyhound. George, the landlord, was always happy to see them, particularly Diane, she being the very well- endowed young lady that she was. It was a few days later. Jamie ordered himself a pint of lager and a Dubonnet and lemonade for Diane. They sat on a two-seater near the fireplace.

'Bit o' bother on t' lock 'smornin'," remarked George, clearly wanting to butt into the young couple's conversation, blatantly attracted by Diane's obvious 'charms'.

'Oh, yeah? What was that then?' asked Jamie in a not particularly interested, go away please, manner.

'Yep. Waterways men pulled a rotting body out.' George said in a matter of fact way. He detected they weren't interested and went back behind his bar.

Jamie went to the bar to order more drinks. George was relaying the morning's excitement to another customer.

'Yep! Police were called an' apparently t' body 'ad been weighted down. Looks like suspicious circumstances.'

'Maybe that's who those guys were that me and Di saw the other day,' offered Jamie.

'Well, if yo' reckon yo' know summat yo' should tell t'coppers.' George instructed.

Up the road at Burton Overy the redecorating of Marsh Cottage had been completed and Helen was informed that she could move in. She was very excited. Firstly she telephoned Wright's Music Shop. It was essential that the Steinway was installed before Ben moved in and she needed to know when it would be delivered. Secondly she telephoned Crowfoot's Carriers a local removal company to ascertain whether they could pick up and deliver the various pieces of furniture she had been amassing over the last week or so. Everything had to be coordinated.

So with everything arranged the removal date was set. The day dawned fair and with Rosemary's assistance Helen threw all her clothes and personal bits and pieces into the back of the Mini and drove the forty-minutes or so to supervise the various removal men and to become a resident of Burton Overy.

Within a week, Helen was settled. There was a place for everything and everything was in its place. Ben had been given notice that he could move as soon as he was ready and a date was fixed. His mother would collect him from his grandparents'. There were tearful goodbyes both from Mabel and her grandson. Even Albert was welling up at one point. Ben was at pains to express his gratitude to his grandparents for everything they had done for him. Helen produced an enormous bunch of flowers for Mabel and with promises of maintaining close contact with regular reciprocal visits Ben and Helen left.

Arriving at Marsh Cottage, Helen showed Ben to his

bedroom where he deposited his suitcase, briefcase and music-case. She then guided him around the house but leaving one particular room until last. Opening the door to the final room she ushered Ben in ahead of her. For Helen, Ben's reaction was a joy to behold. An excitation and reaction of complete surprise closely followed by total disbelief. There it was, a Steinway Boudoir Grand Piano. The finish was so highly polished that one could clearly see one's reflection in it. His incredulity was only surpassed by the magnitude of his grateful and appreciative thanks for something he'd always dreamt of having but never believed he would have. A Steinway Grand!

'Do you like it then?' his mother asked, somewhat needlessly. 'Aren't you going to try it?' Ben sat on the stool and adjusted It to the right height. He lifted the lid and tentatively flexed his fingers before launching into a rendition of Debussy's *Claire de Lune* which brought tears of joy to his mother's eyes.

'Ben, my Ben. I have never ever been happier than I am right at this moment.'

Chapter Forty-Three

Two of British Waterways Board's finest, Ted and Dick, plus a third man, had returned to lock Number 25, this time with a flat-bottomed punt strapped to the roof-rack of their van. The lock was full and the punt was launched. Dick and the third man managed to ease themselves into the punt without it capsizing. Ted opened the paddle in lower gate and slowly, the water content of the lock reduced until the surface of the water was level with the stretch of canal to the Bottom Half-Mile lock Number 26. With the third man steadying the punt against the gate, Dick dropped the grappling iron into the last four feet of water in the lock and it didn't take him long before the flukes of the grappling iron snagged into something.

'I reckon I've a-got summat Ted,' Dick shouted up to his mate on the lockside.

'Well done Dick. Pass us up the rope and I'll gi' yo' a hand haulin' it out.'

The two men heaved on the rope, the third man sat at the further end of the punt in attempt to maintain some equilibrium in the not particularly stable vessel. Slowly they raised a well-rotted hessian sack from the bottom of the lock. Dick managed to pull it into the punt. Whilst it was all but rotten, the sack retained sufficient integrity to still hold some gravel and it was still tied at the top with rope. The other end of the rope was attached to something on the bottom of the lock. Dick now hauled on this rope and slowly a mud-covered, evil-smelling mass broke the surface.

'Bugger me Ted, I can't be sure but I think we might have us a dead body. It don't 'alf stink.'

'I hope you're bloody jokin'.'

''s no joke Ted, look – looks like it might have bin weighted down wi' t' sack. Cor, bloody 'ell it's chuckin' up summat 'orrible. I'll pull 'im in t' punt then I'll cut rope round 'is wrists and you can pull up t' sack, or we'll 'ave too much weight in t' punt and get in a right buggers' muddle."

Dick's plan was executed without mishap if you discount the third man throwing-up at the sight and stench of what was left of a body; a body with very little flesh left on the skull, a skull with the neat round hole in the forehead.

''ang on Ted, 'is feet are tied to more weight.'

Dick managed to recover the second sack, in a similar state to the first and Ted hauled that one onto the quayside as well. He then closed the paddles in the lower end gates and opened those in the upper gates and the lock slowly filled. The punt rose up in the lock where it was then a simple but far from straightforward affair to drag the remains on to the lockside.

The third man, with colour returning to his face, had been to the van and returned with a flask of tea. He stood looking at what they'd recovered from the lock.

'Shall us check that's done t' trick then?' said the third man swilling tea around in his mouth but nevertheless mindful that their task had been to clear the blockage which was impeding the flow of water through the paddle.

'I reckon we should call coppers first. We can check t' lock while we wait for 'em to get 'ere.' Dick was clearly the 'gaffer' and was exerting his seniority. 'I'll drive up t' village and find a phone box. Won't need no money, I reckon this is a 999.'

While he was gone Ted shared a cup of tea from the third man's flask and then they emptied the lock to check the operation of the paddle and confirmed that they had indeed cleared the blockage; a blockage of a kind they were certainly not expecting.

After about an hour a Wolseley 6/99 police car arrived followed by a Morris Minor panda-car with blue light flashing. The two police vehicles were followed a few minutes later by an unmarked black van. The senior officer introduced himself as Detective Inspector Mosely and with him, Detective Constable Cartwright. They both flashed their warrant cards. From the panda, emerged a uniformed constable, and a plain-clothed photographer. Two men from the black van stood by with a stretcher and a body-bag. Just above the lock, the *Sheldrake* was waiting to work her way through. Pat Henderson, the boatman and his lad were taking a keen interest in what was going on beside the lock.

Chapter Forty-Four

After the incident at Top Half-Mile Lock Jock had finally completed servicing the Russell Newbery and with Helen having abandoned him for good, he had managed to turn the *Emily Rose* around at Kilby Wharf and head straight back from whence he came. He was all too well aware that now more than ever he needed to keep a very low profile. He had committed four murders and the illegal business no longer had any stock with which to trade. Jock's only assets were an Ariel 350, registered to a dead man, untaxed and uninsured, a seventy-two foot narrowboat and a six-figure bank account. He knew that it wouldn't be very long before the police would be breathing down his neck. He wanted to get back to Foxton. He was known at Foxton and by a certain type of person not dissimilar to himself who lived on the periphery of the underworld and upon whom he could rely to get him out of a scrape; in return for a 'handshake'. However whilst getting back to Foxton ordinarily would not be a problem with just a dozen locks and some lovely countryside, there were a couple of issues of which Jock was very nervous. The first of these was getting through the Top Half-Mile lock at Newton. He knew what lay at the bottom of lock and how it came to lie there. Did anyone else? The second issue which intimidated him into a state of terror was the Saddington Tunnel. Yes, he knew it was irrational. Yes, he knew he was now paranoid about it but just the thought of it brought him out in a cold sweat.

The *Emily Rose* navigated her way up through locks 29 to 26. On leaving 26 the palpitations set in. The gates of 25 were against him. He jumped ashore, and loosely secured the boat whilst he made the lock ready. With one paddle raised he moved to the other. No longer was there just a mere trickle through. Now there was a veritable torrent. He had a pretty good idea why. The 'blockage' must have been cleared. He wondered if anyone else had noticed. Surely? He brought the boat through, dropped the paddles and vowed never to come this way again.

Jock was cold, he was hungry, he was tired. He gently took *Emily Rose* into the bank and secured the boat with warps fore and aft. He had decided to stop after the Kibworth Top Lock. He needed to sleep, eat and get warm. He lit the stove, put on an extra sweater, heated and devoured a tin of soup and lay down. His next demon was not far away but he could not bring himself to confront it.

It was several days later when *Sheldrake* came up through the Kibworth locks. *Emily Rose* was still tied up. The boatman on the *Sheldrake*, Patrick, gave Jock a hail.

''ey up there Jock. Yo' in trouble mate? Yo' was tied up there when I come up two days ago.' It was as if Jock had lost track of time.

'Och, Pat – it's yersel'. Ahm OK, but the bloody water pump impeller's gone. Ahm waiting fur one t' be delivered." Telling lies was second nature to Jock.

'Can I gi' yo' a tow?'

'Tha' s very kind but I got a bloke comin' doon the towpath tae find me wi' a spare. He'll be here in a while I should think." Always one for a bit of gossip Pat launched into a description of what he'd witnessed at the Top Half Mile.

'Did yo' 'ear 'ows they pulled a rotten body an' a couple o' sacks out o' Number 25 this morning. I reckon that's why the bloody paddle were so slow."

Jock started to panic. 'Pull yer'sel t'gither man.' He urged himself to respond

'Did was he?' His response lacked surprise.

'Dead? I should bloody say so. Shot through 'is 'ead so it seems. Bin in the lock for years the coppers reckon.'

'Och.' It was the only response Jock could muster.

'Any road up, if yo're sure yo' don't want a tow, I'm off. Tara-a-bit.'

'I'll catch ye at Foxton. Cheers' was all Jock could manage. 'Ok then, if yo're sure, OK."

Sheldrake pottered on. Pat the boatman gave him a wave.

'What to do, what to do?' thought Jock. He considered getting the Ariel on to the towpath and riding off. He wouldn't need the boat anymore. He could just leave it here. 'Not practical. Where would I go?' he thought. 'I can go anywhere! I've got money!' he reminded himself. After further consideration, he was back to Plan A, Foxton. He just had to get through the blasted tunnel.

He poured himself a stiff whisky and tried to mentally prepare himself for the Saddington ordeal. He took the Luger from the waistband of his trousers and laid it where it would be instantly available if he needed it. He started the Russell Newbery; reliable as ever and waited until the *Sheldrake* had disappeared into the tunnel. Jock tended to his warps, put the gearbox into ahead and moved into the midstream. Within a few minutes the entrance to the tunnel loomed large, like a great black hole waiting to swallow him.

Not a great deal, if anything, was known about light speed singularities and mass time dilation in 1964. The existence of a space–time continuum or closed time curve where two points in time allow travel between them through an invisible gateway was not a very frequent or popular topic of conversation either.

It had started to rain. *Emily Rose* slowly drew into the Saddington Tunnel. It was pitch black. The Russell Newbery gave a cough and died. Jock was about to curse but the sudden and rapid drop in temperature took his breath away. Instantaneously there was a totally blinding, incandescent flash of blue light accompanied by an ear-piercing oscillation of high frequencies. A few seconds. All went quiet. As his pupils dilated and his sight partially returned but as if through an out-of-focus haze, Jock thought he could detect steam rising from the water. Then there was light at the end of the tunnel or was there?

'Where am I?" he screamed. The engine restarted as if by a mind of its own and *Emily Rose* gently emerged from the tunnel and into the sunshine of an early winter's afternoon. There was no one on board.

Chapter Forty-Five

Life at Marsh Cottage could not have been more pleasant for either Helen or Ben. They were more akin to friends rather than mother and son. Helen had put 'L' plates on the Mini and Ben was driving to and from school under his mother's supervision. When he was not at school Ben spent his time between homework, piano practice, seeing Tina, and in (or out) with his mother. Not necessarily in that order nor in equal measure. On Saturdays Ben and Helen would do the shopping together. Ben would then visit his grandparents whilst Helen called in to see Frank at the farm.

The normal form for Ben and Tina on a Saturday evening was a visit to the cinema. This particular Saturday whilst queuing to see *A Shot in the Dark* starring Peter Sellers and Elke Sommer, they bumped into Jamie and Diane.

'I'm looking forward to this' said Tina excitedly. 'It'll be so much more entertaining than last week.'

'What'd you see last week then?' asked Diane.

'*Becket* – thought we should – it's part of our 'A' level syllabus. Didn't think much of the film but Peter O'Toole is lovely!' Tina giggled. The small talk continued.

They sat together at the back of the cinema and after the film Jamie offered them a lift home in his Triumph Herald.

'That'd be great,' said Ben 'but I've moved now. I'm now living with my mum in Burton Overy.'

'Burton Overy,' repeated Jamie, 'that's the next village to Great Glen isn't it, near where we used to go trainspotting?'

Ben gave a short resume of recent events and took delight in announcing that he was now having driving lessons and had been promised a car of his own for his eighteenth.

'Well, look, me and Di quite often go to a pub in Great Glen, the Old Greyhound. Do you know it?'

Tina was anxiously looking at her watch and trying to get a word in.

'Sorry, but I've got to dash otherwise I'll miss my last bus.'

'OK, got to go Jamie sorry, nice to see you again Diane. We'll get together again soon – maybe see you in that pub.'

It was getting close to Christmas. Helen had decided, in consultation with Ben, that they would host a Christmas party at Marsh Cottage. Amongst the guests Helen wished to invite were Kate and Stuart. Ben wasn't sure who Kate was. He had no idea who Stuart was, until his mother explained.

'After your dad left me I had nowhere to go. Frank, you know Frank, arranged for me to stay in one of his brother Ernie's farm cottages. Kate, is Ernie's daughter and she was your baby sitter – looked after you as if you were her own. I don't know where I'd have been without Ernie and Kate, or Frank, come to that.'

'And Stuart?'

'Oh yes, Stuart is Kate's husband. They got married a few months ago.'

Kate and Stuart had moved to live in Fleckney after their wedding although Kate still managed the farm at Kilby Bridge for her dad. They had taken to walking their Labrador 'Byron' by the canal on a Sunday morning, one way or the other, upstream or down. This particular day it was crisp. There had been a frost and the air was clear and bright, in fact a lovely morning for a walk. They took the horse path over the top of Saddington Tunnel with Byron running ahead, sniffing out this and that as dogs do. As they came near to getting back onto the actual towpath, they could see a narrowboat which seemed to have run aground on the mud by the bank of the canal. As they approached closer, the boat's name could be clearly seen; it was the *Emily Rose*. Stuart shouted.

'Hello, anybody aboard?' No reply. He climbed aboard himself, getting his boots muddy in the process. The cabin door was open and he stood at the top of the companionway steps and shouted down into cabin.

'Anyone in?' No reply. Then he noticed it. On a small shelf just at the top of the companionway. The gun. Stuart's instincts told him this was not right, this was suspicious.

'Kate, run along to Smeeton Road bridge, find a phone and call the police.' His words carried a sense of urgency. 'Stop a car if you need to. Tell the police there's a narrowboat here on the mud in suspicious circumstances. There's no one on board but there is a gun. I think it's a Luger.'

'Whatever for?' Kate hadn't seen the gun, nor did she find it particularly strange that here was a perfectly good narrowboat, seemingly abandoned on the mud. But one of the reasons she had married Stuart was for his eminent common sense so she ran along as she had been instructed. It was only about twenty minutes before there was a log jam of police cars on Smeeton Road bridge. There were policemen and women everywhere; plainclothes, uniform, dog-handlers, the towpath was being overrun. Leading the charge was Detective Inspector Mosely, warrant card held high. He approached a slightly apprehensive Stuart.

'Was it you that phoned it in?'

'No, I sent my wife to call you.'

'Well done! This could be the break we've been waiting for!'

Mosely's sidekick handed him a loudhailer through which the Detective Inspector issued his instructions to the gathering forces of constabulary. The ranks dispersed hither and thither. DI Mosely and DC Cartwright boarded the boat.

'There's a footprint here sir,' observed Cartwright.

'Ah sorry, that'll be mine. I trod in the mud I'm afraid,' apologised Stuart.

'No matter' said Mosely. 'We've got the gun here Cartwright and I'll bet my pension it's the murder weapon.'

The DI took a handkerchief from his pocket and used it to pick up the Luger which he then dropped into an evidence bag being offered by his Detective Constable.

'Did you handle the gun?' he asked Stuart.

'No I didn't. Can you tell me what's going on?'

The DI addressed his DC.

'Cartwright, give Mr erm, Mr...'

'Cross, Stuart Cross.'

'Give Mr Cross an idea of what's going on and get some details from him. We'll need a statement later.'

With that, Kate and Byron had made their way back, through a cordon of uniformed officers, and returned the way they came. Stuart remained to listen to DC Cartwright.

Chapter Forty-Six

With Christmas and the festive season approaching, George, landlord of the Old Greyhound in Great Glen, possibly more in hope than expectation had advertised for temporary bar staff. He was as pleased as punch when Diane asked she could have the job. A pretty girl with such wonderful 'assets' behind the bar would be sure to attract custom.

School had broken up for the holidays. Ben was grateful for that as he'd grown just a little weary of accompanying Christmas Carols. The rather more exciting news was that Mr Sims had suggested that he was ready for the 'big time'.

'Associate Performance Diploma for you next term, I think.' Ben was flattered that his teacher should think him capable.

'Then perhaps we might look at presenting a public concert performance.' Whilst he had great respect for Mr Sims Ben did wonder whether the notion of a concert was a step too far. Still, he had told his mother of the ambitions that his mentor had for him and Helen was thrilled. She was so proud of her son.

'Well, this calls for a celebration,' Helen said. 'Ring Tina, tell her we'll pick her up in half-an-hour, then get your coat."

Half-an-hour later, the Mini, driven by Ben, pulled up

outside the Red Lion, and Tina was just saying goodbye to her dad. She was already familiar with Ben's news.

'Well, where are we going then?' asked Tina.

'I thought we'd go to that pub in Great Glen. Looks nice, and we've driven passed it enough times without going in,' Helen replied.

Ben parked the Mini and went into the pub. It was fairly busy mainly with middle-aged men crowded around the bar like flies round the jam jar! Diane looked up from the pint she was pulling when she heard the front door close.

'Ben Blake!' she exclaimed in greeting. Ben waved with a surprised look on his face.

George, at the other end of the bar had heard the shout and hurried over to Diane.

'Did you say Ken Blake?' he asked with a degree of urgency. By now, Ben had hung up his coat and was at the bar. He overheard George's question to Diane and answered on her behalf.

'No, Ben Blake' he emphasised. 'Ken was my father. Sadly, he's no longer with us. He died.' He gestured in the direction of his mum,

'And this is my mother, Helen. Ken's widow.' George was momentarily flustered.

'We'd better sit down and have a chat, Mrs Blake, Ben.'

Neither of them had any idea what it could be that this complete stranger wanted to talk to them about. George spoke directly to Tina posing his question in a somewhat patronising manner.

'Are yo' one o' t' family, sweetheart?'

'No, not yet anyway.' That made Ben blush.

'Then if yo' don't mind goin' and getting some drink? Tell Di 'George said it's on t' house'.' Tina felt just a bit miffed about being excluded, but at least it gave her the opportunity to have a bit of a girly talk with Diane.

George didn't know quite where to start. He looked at Ben then at Helen.

'Now, I might 'ave this all wrong, and if I 'ave, I'm sorry I'm sure.'

'Carry on,' said Helen.

'Well, more an' a few years ago, a fella stayed here. 'is name were Ken Blake. Nice bloke. 'ad a beard. 'e asked me if I could look after a box for 'im while' e went to Scotland. Well more like a crate than a box, y' know, like a packing crate.' Helen and Ben were transfixed by George's narrative.

'It were all locked up wi' a padlock an' everything and we put it in one o' my stables, out back. Took four on us to lift it! Any road up, it's still there an' I'd quite like it shifted out the bloody way. I don't want the responsibility. 'e paid me a bit for storage, but that were years ago.' Ben's curiosity was getting the better of him.

'What's in it, this crate?'

'I've no idea. It's locked. It weighs a bloody ton. If it is your 'usband's missus, do you mind taking it away? I'll be glad to see back o' it.'

'Can you remember exactly when the crate was left here?' Helen asked.

'Not long after t' war. It were delivered by a couple o' soldiers in an army truck.'

It was arranged that Ben and Helen would come to the pub the following day to inspect the crate. There could be some mistake regarding ownership, but Helen thought it highly unlikely. In fact she secretly knew full well that this was Ken's alright. But what were the contents?

The following lunchtime, Ben, Helen, and Frank, who Helen had phoned earlier and got him there under the pretext of a Christmas drink, were shown to the stable by George. George unlocked the stable door. In the corner was a large pile of sacks and assorted rubbish covered with muck and cobwebs. The sacks and other stuff were shoved to the ground and the wooden crate was revealed under almost eighteen years' worth of dust and detritus. Frank took three or four attempts to blow the dust away after which everyone could make out the label stencilled on the lid. 'Sgt Kenneth Blake QM' c/o The Old Greyhound, Great Glen, Leicester'. The title 'Blake & McClean EuroBankInst' was stencilled on the side of the crate. There were also some other labels, one in German, and one in Russian which no one present could make head nor tale of but it didn't matter.

'Oh yes, this is Ken's, he told me before he died that he was expecting it. I'd forgotten all about it. I'll have it collected tomorrow George. Will £50 cover the outstanding storage costs?' Ben looked at his mother wondering what she was up to. Why the secrecy and the untruths all of a sudden? What were the secrets of the box? Helen looked at Frank and gave him a wink and nod. Frank looked at Ben at gave him a nod and a wink.

'Yes, £50 will be fine missus thank you kindly. Glad t' be rid o' it. Only sorry your 'usband is no longer wi' us. Let's all go in, Drinks on t' house."

The stable was relocked and the four of them went into the pub. 'Courage, Vigilance, Fidelty' Ben read on the sign.

Chapter Forty-Seven

It didn't take long for the forensics report to reach Detective Inspector Mosely's desk. There was no doubt in Mosely's mind that the bullet that killed the man in lock 25 had been fired from the Luger found on the *Emily Rose*. The forensics report wasn't quite so positive though. But who had fired the gun? This was less certain. The last registration of the old Ariel 350 motorbike found on the narrowboat had been to a Ronald Nicholls of an address in Hinckley. Enquiries so far had revealed that Mr Nicholls' neighbours hadn't seen him for years. An elderly gentleman was answering DC Cartwright's questions.

'I've lived here since before the war and I reckon it must have been soon after that we last saw Ron. Nice enough young bloke. Used to ride a motorbike he bought from the land-army. After a couple of years or so, the landlord had the house emptied and done up. Been three or four different tenants since then. I do remember at the time, a bloke from the Midland Red came round looking for him. He used to work on the buses as a conductor I reckon. Up early, in late... I seem to remember, now I'm thinking about it, his driver disappeared at about the same time; bloke they called Jock.'

That name again!

DC Cartwright's next stop was at the Midland Red depot but there was no one there who could recall Ron Nicholls or 'Jock'. DI Mosely was almost pleased with the results of his DC's enquiries so far. He was beginning to put the jigsaw together.

'Ok Cartwright, get yourself down the canal. See what you can find out about that boat.'

Having been notified of an abandoned boat, the British Waterways Board had instructed the senior lockkeeper at Foxton, to organise a tow, just to get the boat out of harm's way. The senior lockkeeper at Foxton had made contact with his counterpart in Leicester to instruct the next boat coming up to take the *Emily Rose* in tow and deliver her to Foxton.

DC Cartwright was somewhat surprised when he arrived at the Smeeton Road bridge to discover that the boat was no longer there. He rang his DI who wasn't best pleased with this news.

'Don't they know it's a possible crime scene? This might well be a murder enquiry. It is a bloody murder enquiry! We'll have bloody muddy boots all over everywhere... if there's any evidence it'll be contaminated....' he went on and on a bit, and Cartwright held the receiver away from his ear. His boss was going off on one; not for the first time.

'Ok Cartwright, use your initiative if you've got any. Find that bloody boat and keep people off it.' The DC did have initiative and it wasn't very long before he'd traced the *Emily Rose*. She'd been seen under tow on her way towards Foxton where there were boat chandlery services and other 'facilities'. When he arrived at Foxton *Emily Rose* was being made fast to the quay outside the Foxton Locks Inn. Using a roll of police 'Do Not Cross' tape Cartwright did his best to warn people away and cordon off the area of the quay where the boat was moored. Given that this was right outside the pub the tape had the opposite effect and on-lookers and spectators were drawn to it out of curiosity.

The senior lockkeeper was senior not just in his standing with the Waterways Board, but in years as well. Perhaps he should have been retired years ago. He tapped the DC on his shoulder as he was tying off one end of his tape.

'I'm Fred, the lockkeeper 'ere at Foxton. What's happened? Where's Jock?'

That name again!

Mention of the name 'Jock' set off all the bells and whistles in Cartwright's brain.

'Where's the nearest phone I can use? I must call the inspector. This is urgent!'

About forty minutes later the Wolseley 6/99, blue light flashing, roared over the Gumley Road bridge and drew up as close to the *Emily Rose* as tourists, trippers and Joe Public would allow. The imposing figure of Detective Inspector Mosely stepped from the car followed by a uniformed constable adjusting his cap. Mosely, Cartwright and Fred disappeared into the lockkeeper's office whilst the constable stood on duty protecting the integrity of the crime scene, if there was any left.

With what he considered to be some astute police work, it was Mosely's contention that Fred should know the owner of the *Emily Rose*. Surely, he would have checked the boat up and down the Foxton Flight many times? Under questioning Fred had little option than to reveal all he knew about Jock, which in truth was not very much. He was economical with the any detail and let on precious little about Jock's 'activities'. He was also shrewd and wily enough not to implicate himself in any way when it came to the black market sales. Fred, exercising his notion of prudence, also neglected accidentally on purpose to mention the young woman who had lived and worked on board *Emily Rose* for years. Like Frank, Fred had a very soft spot for Helen, and he wouldn't want to see her in trouble.

So with a few more pieces of the puzzle in place Mosely was now firmly convinced that Nicholls had been murdered by Jock, whoever he might be – a Scotsman, presumably. And Jock who had been involved in some buying and selling, possibly of an illegal nature, had disappeared into thin air. The CID officers decided that whilst they were here, they should take a look on board and search the vessel. They didn't really have much of a clue about what they might be looking for and in consequence discovered little of any great interest to assist with their enquiries. They did although take away the ledger of sales and cash receipts such as it was, which Jock had begun to keep in the early days of his enterprise. Had they looked a little more diligently they would have found a wooden box. Had they looked in the wooden box, they would have found a large quantity of cash; a very, very large quantity of cash.

As the police officers were about to leave Foxton, Fred was advised that the boat was still under investigation and the police would make contact if he was needed to assist with their enquiries. In the meantime, should 'Jock' turn up, or if he, Fred, or anyone else connected with the canals could provide any further information on the man or his whereabouts, they should telephone, immediately. The Detective Inspector handed Fred his card with his direct line number. As soon as the Wolseley and its occupants had disappeared, Fred tore the card into small pieces and threw them into the canal.

Chapter Forty-Eight

It was the morning of Christmas Eve. Frank had turned up in the Jaguar towing a small trailer. After coffee had been served at Marsh Cottage Helen, Frank and Ben, drove down to Great Glen and the Old Greyhound. Frank very skilfully reversed the trailer close to the stable block drawing an admiring glance from Ben as he did so. The pub was not open yet so Helen went to the private entrance at the back. Frank dropped the tailgate on the trailer and he and Ben were waiting by the stables when Ben noticed the Triumph Herald in the carpark.

'It looks like Jamie's here. I guess he's dropping Diane off. Could be useful, if we need a hand.'

George had obviously had the same thought since Jamie did indeed follow Helen and George out of the pub and over to the stables. George opened the stable door and the four men heaved, shoved, pushed and pulled the crate into a position where they could all get a grip and lift it out of the stable and into the trailer. The trailer sank down on its springs with the weight. George stood panting. Frank closed the tailgate. Helen handed over five £10 notes to George.

'I hope yo'll come an' join us for one over Christmas?' The invitation was more of a question.

'We almost certainly will, thanks.' Ben quite fancied the

prospect of sitting in the pub with Tina and his old train-spotting mate.

Frank drove back to Burton Overy and there was much speculation during the short trip as to the contents of the crate. When they arrived back at the cottage, Frank again demonstrated his expertise and reversed the trailer into the narrow space by the side of the cottage. The crate was far too heavy for Frank and Ben to lift without assistance so Helen suggested they open it where it was in the trailer and take the contents into the cottage a bit at a time. Frank took a crowbar from the boot of his car and without too much difficulty prised the padlock off.

'Do you remember the last time you did that for me?' Helen asked.

'I most certainly do. One o' the biggest surprises of my life it were,' recalled Frank.

Carefully, Frank eased the crowbar between the lid and the side of the crate and levered it ajar. The nails creaked as they were partially withdrawn from where they'd been hammered eighteen years previously. Ben had taken a clawhammer from Frank's toolkit and was now assisting by prising out the nails. The crate was certainly well secured. It was quite a while before the lid was finally removed. Ben and Frank peered in. Helen looked on. Straw was tightly packed around whatever was inside. Frank reached in and put his hands around something solid. He pulled it from the crate.

'Bugger me!' exclaimed Frank. 'Sorry about me language.' He handed it to Ben.

'Bugger me!' exclaimed Ben. He handed it to Helen.

'Bugger me as well!' exclaimed Helen. 'It' was a solid gold bar.

Frank reached into the crate a second time and pulled out a second gold bar, then a third and a fourth.

'Wouldn't it be a good idea to get these indoors out o' sight before we get any more out?'

The unloading continued until the crate was empty. In the sitting room of the cottage was a neatly stacked pile of forty gold bars.

'However much are they worth?' asked Ben. Neither Frank nor Helen had any idea.

'What are we going to do with them?' asked Ben. Neither Frank nor Helen had any idea.

They stood looking at the hoard disbelieving what they were looking at; the three of them in a state of fascinated wonderment. Eventually Helen suggested maybe she should cover them with something until the next step was determined. She found a tablecloth from a drawer and threw it over the stack. Smoothing out the creases, she then placed the fruit bowl on top.

'There you are,' she said proudly. 'The most expensive occasional table in the world!'

It was generally agreed that the occasional table would need to be moved before the Christmas party gathering, if only to free up some floor space so it was hidden around the house, one or two bars here and there. Helen made some sandwiches and as Ben and Frank ate, she attempted to contextualise how this new-found wealth had come about. It was inconceivable to Ben that so much of his dad's background was bound up in a smokescreen of black market dealings and clandestine operations through which he had managed to manipulate the army and turn the war to his own advantage. The stencilled wording on the crate had not gone unnoticed by Frank at least. He pleaded with Helen to assure him, and Ben, that whatever its basis may have been, her relationship with Duncan McClean was now over for good.

'So, dad had a partner in this bloke McClean?' Helen

answered as truthfully as she dared. She even went so far as to amplify what little detail she had already given her son regarding her own part in Jock McClean's business when he was a baby.

'It was wrong I know. In fact it was worse than wrong. It was totally unforgiveable, yet I hope that one day you may find it in your heart to forgive me.' Then as if in mitigation but by no means in a reproachful manner, Helen added, 'Where do you think all the money came from? This house, the Mini, the Steinway? Where do you think the money for your new car is going to come from?' All rhetorical questions perhaps, but Ben hadn't previously given them any thought. Frank sat silently. He was really hoping that the 'root of all evil' was not about to jeopardise the relationship between the two people he cared most about in the whole world.

'And now we've got a whole lot more!' Ben was almost gleeful, and the atmosphere lightened at a stroke. Helen was relieved and delighted with the way in which Ben had reacted. She now had a co-conspirator as well as a co-beneficiary.

'But mum, if dad and you were in partnership with this Jock bloke is he not going to come looking for his share?' Ben asked the question the answer to which Frank had also been wrestling with. Frank looked intently at Helen. Much depended on her answer.

'He may do, I really don't know. I don't know what the arrangement was with your dad for instance. I mean Jock disposed of all the stuff we moved into Frank's barn; the stuff that Frank got arrested for. Did your dad get a share of that profit, or did I get your dad's share as well? I really don't know. Is Jock expecting a half share of this Nazi gold? I don't know. But, just in case, we'll put some aside. What I do know is that I haven't seen Jock since a couple of weeks after your dad was…' She hesitated. Did Ben need to know that Ken had been murdered? '… since a couple of weeks after dad died, at the funeral. What's more, I never want to see Jock ever him again' There was relief all round, and the sandwiches were all gone.

Chapter Forty-Nine

The party on Boxing Day was a splendid affair. Everyone that had been invited turned up and thoroughly enjoyed themselves. Albert spent most of the time deep in conversation with Uncle John. Mabel wanted to know all there was to know about Tina. Rosemary, Neville, Charlie and Frank sat in the kitchen drinking and talking, and the topics of conversation were getting more hilarious with every drink. Frank and Ernie sat by the inglenook, the log fire supplemented incidentally with the wood from the crate lending not only warmth but atmosphere. Helpfully the fug from St Bruno was going straight up the chimney too. Sid was walking round taking photographs of everything and everyone with his new camera.

Ben, was getting acquainted with his former sitter, 'Aunty' Kate. Stuart was telling him the tale of how they had found a narrowboat on the mud, the Luger and everything, and how it had led to the arrival of the 'entire Leicestershire Constabulary' to investigate.

'Stuart, don't exaggerate! You've had enough!' chided his wife. They all laughed and poured yet more wine anyway. All afternoon Helen had been running around topping up glasses, proffering sausage rolls, ham sandwiches, vol-au-vents, cheese straws. What a party!

The following day, after he and Tina had helped his mum clear up, Ben announced that they were going for a walk. Helen didn't mind, preferring to sit a snooze in front of the television. There was a Polish film she wanted to watch, *The Yellow Slippers* and then on BBC2, Malcolm Sargent was conducting the Royal Liverpool Philharmonic in a performance of *The Messiah*. Tina was grateful for the chance to escape from the house for a while. They walked to Great Glen and the Old Greyhound. Being the evening after two days of Christmas festivities, the pub was quiet. George was having a night off and Diane was running the bar when she wasn't stood taking to Jamie, sat on a barstool at one end of it. There was something genuine about the affection with which they greeted each other. A short while passed, and Ben took Jamie to one side, leaving Tina talking to Di.

'There's something I'd like your help with, if you can.'

'Sure, whatever.'

'This is all very secret, promise me not a word. Do you reckon your dad might know the price of gold?' Jamie gave Ben a funny look.

'Gold what?'

'No, gold, like in gold bars.'

'Where'd you get…' before he could finish the question Ben had answered.

'That crate that had come for my dad.'

'I'll ask him. He knows about most things – or thinks he does anyway!'

'There's another thing as well. Have you heard anything about an abandoned narrowboat?'

'Me and Di saw some Waterways blokes at Newton Top Half Mile Lock a week or so back. George reckons they found a body… could that be anything to do with it?'

'It might. Can you keep your ear to the ground and let me know.'

'Yeah, for sure. What's all this about?'

'I'll let you know when I know.'

'OK. All this information's going to cost you a pint – lager please!'

Piano practice had slipped down the agenda a little over the festive period and with a performance diploma and possible concert to prepare for Ben was only too well aware how important it was. So he introduced a self-imposed regime of practise mornings and evenings. Afternoons were generally spent with Tina, walking or having a driving lesson. It was hard to believe how much his life had changed in so few months. The death of his dad was a distant memory now but the occasional aching fingers on his right hand after a three -hour practise session were a reminder of that fateful day.

Having completed his stint on the piano one lunchtime in January, Jamie pulled up in his Triumph. Ben went to the front door to let him in.

'I won't come in, probably better if you came with me anyway, I have some news.'

Ben put his coat on, gave his mum a peck on the cheek and drove off with Jamie. It seemed appropriate to go to their old favourite spot by the canal and railway at Newton Bridge.

'I had a word with my dad without being specific and in a roundabout way got him to get in touch with one of his mates on the council who knows someone who knows someone else, you know, about the gold market. Apparently a standard gold bar weighs one kilogram, which is two-point-two pounds. If you were buying from a dealer or the Royal Mint one bar would cost you between five and six thousand pounds.'

'Wow!'

'Hold on if you're selling it's probably going to be less and the price fluctuates depending on World Money Markets and all sorts of shit that dad tried to explain but I didn't have a clue what he was on about.'

'Yeah, but even so, say at five-thousand…' Ben was doing the arithmetic in his head.

'You said you got one from that crate.' Jamie reminded him.

'One what?'

'A gold bar, dummy!'

'No,' replied Ben, 'we've got forty!'

'Bloody hell!'

Right at that moment with an impeccable sense of timing, a Class 40 diesel charged passed. They looked at each other and by this completely uncanny coincidence they both collapsed into paroxysms of delirious laughter. When they'd both calmed down, Jamie also delivered on the other line of enquiry requested by Ben.

'Sometimes useful having an old man with connections. He's in the Masons you know, whatever that is – a sort of secret society for old blokes from what I can make out. Anyway this bloke Mosely is in the same lodge as my dad."

'What's the 'lodge'?'

'I think it's like a branch. There are different branches all over.'

'And who is this Mosely bloke?'

'He's a copper – a Detective Inspector. He was telling my dad and some other members in the lodge about a case he's on. Remember I told you about the Waterways men at the lock?" Ben nodded, "Well, apparently, they did pull out a stiff, except he wasn't stiff. He was all but rotted. They reckon he's a murder victim on account of the bullet hole through his skull and that he was shot about seventeen years ago. Then it seems they only went and found the gun – a German World War Two Luger.'

'What in the lock as well?'

'No, on a narrowboat – an abandoned narrowboat called *Emily Rose*. Mosely's certain the gun, the Luger's the murder weapon. How about that mate?'

'Bloody hell!'

Ben sat back and digested what he'd just been told. He was mightily impressed with Jamie's investigative prowess and the information he had uncovered.

'Does he know where the boat is now?' asked Ben.

'I think he said Foxton. Why?' Ben gave Jamie a very brief synopsis of his mum's involvement with the Scotsman and the black market business on the narrowboat; of how his dad and the Scotsman were partners and somehow looted the gold shipment from the Germans during the war. He went to great lengths to impress upon Jamie just how quintessentially confidential all this information must be, or they'd all be in trouble, or worse, in gaol.

'This Scotsman, wasn't called Jock by any chance?' Jamie asked.

'All Scotsmen get call Jock!'

'Mosely, the copper reckons the murderer was called Jock.'

They both sat in silence. Jamie lit a cigarette and Ben was wrestling with the information, the intelligence, his friend had uncovered and what the possible implications might be as far as the Blake family was involved. He urgently needed to talk to his mum.

'Shall I run you home now?'

'Yes please mate. I really need to talk to my mum and I reckon I owe you more than one pint of lager. Could you drink a gold bar's worth?'

Chapter Fifty

Ben was disturbed by what he had heard; not just disturbed, troubled and worried. He sat at home staring into the middle distance at nothing, trying to make sense of it all and how his mother and he might be implicated. Helen came into the room and sat down with a magazine.

'Penny for them?'

'Sorry?'

'Penny for your thoughts?'

Ben told his mum everything that Jamie had told him and how the information had come from a reliable source. Helen clearly shared Ben's concern.

'I think we should go to Foxton and check the boat; make sure there's nothing on there that might connect me too closely to Jock. I'd rather not be accused of being an accessory to murder.' She recalled those few moments after Ken had stepped on to the boat and thought of how Jock had disposed of Ken's body. Helen was in no doubt whatsoever that her erstwhile husband had been murdered, and that Jock was the murderer. She also concluded that Ken wasn't Jock's first victim either.

'Do the police have any idea here Jock is?'

'Jamie didn't mention it. I imagine maybe that his dad might well be kept up-to-date by the Inspector at his lodge meetings though.'

Ben and Jamie took the Mini to Foxton. Ben drove, it was driving lesson time after all. They left the car on the side of the Gumley Road. Helen could see her distinctive decorations of the *Emily Rose* and they walked down towards the boat beside the flight of locks. Sitting on a beer crate outside the Foxton Locks Inn was a familiar face.

'Fred! How good to see you. How are you?'

Fred looked up from the whittling that was occupying his attention.

'Helen? Is that you?'

They embraced like old friends, which is of course what they were after all the time Helen had lived on the boat whilst it was moored right where it was. She couldn't help but notice the police tape.

'I see we've had visitors,' she observed.

'We 'ave that. But I told 'im nowt. 'e were looking for Jock but I ain't seen 'im since the pair o' you took off six months since.'

'Who's 'e?' Helen asked, just wishing to verify Jamie's facts.

''tective somebody. Mosel'? Summat like that. Pompous bugger. I dint tell 'im owt about you, honest I dint. 'sfar as 'e knows, Jock were on' is own.'

'Thanks Fred you're a star. Can I show my son around the boat please?'

'Yer son eh? Can't see why not – 'tis your boat after all 'sfar as I'm concerned, what, wi' Jock nowhere to be found.'

Ben and Helen ducked under the police tape and went aboard, down into the cabin. Helen had a good rummage around. Apart from some of Jock's clothes there was no evidence of herself. She was mightily relieved to not have found anything to connect her to the boat. Even so, she did give a few handles and surfaces a cursory wipe in case there might be any discernible fingerprints left behind. She uncovered the hold a little way and climbed in. It was empty apart from a very sad looking excuse of a motorbike propped on its stand. Back in the cabin with the hold re-covered, she went directly to a hidden compartment beneath the companionway steps, behind the Russell Newbery engine. She withdrew a wooden box. Finally satisfied that there was nothing to connect her with the boat, they returned to the quay, Ben carrying the box.

'Fred, how would I go about selling this boat so that it can't be traced to me?'

'Is it yours to sell though? 'ave yo' got a bill o' sale or proof o' ownership?'

'No.'

''as Jock?'

'I very much doubt that!'

'Thought as much. Well, in that case, yo'll need a dodgy brokerage.'

'Do you know one?'

'Ah, c'mon now 'elen, is a pig pork, what do yo' reckon? Do yo' want to leave it wi' me? I can take care o' it for you. Yo' won't get much of a price mind, through the bloke I know.'

'Fred, whatever you get, you keep. I just want all trace of it gone. A fresh paint job and a new name as well which I'll pay for. Let me know how much.'

'I understand. It'll be no problem an' all under the radar, don't yo' be worryin'.'

'Fred, you're an angel. Thank you.'

'Welcome! Yo' look after yer mam now boy!'

Ben carried the wooden box back to the car and on the drive back he asked how she could sell the boat when Jock might be back for it.

'He won't.' Helen's answer was quite categorical. "He's the suspect in a murder enquiry, he's been involved in all manner of illegal dealings, and now he's disappeared. The first place the police will be looking for him is on that boat. I remember him telling me that he bought the boat because he could hide it in remote spots of the canal network. He won't be back, I'll guarantee it. He's many things but he's not stupid.'

Ben safely navigated the car back to Burton and they had tea.

'What's in the box mum?'

'Why don't you take a look?'

Ben looked. Where his mum was concerned his lessons in learning to expect the unexpected were quite well advanced. The contents of the box were the next lesson. He lifted the lid to reveal a staggeringly mind-boggling amount of cash. Notes of all denominations were just crammed in there. Some had been sorted, some in rolls, some in bundles, but it appeared that whoever was sorting got fed up with the exercise, there being so much money, and just stuffed it in the box and forced the lid down.

'Jock's?' Ben enquired. His mum nodded.

'Jock's!' affirmed his mum. 'Once a month we'd split the proceeds from everything we had sold between us – after taking out costs and expenses of course. This box is Jock's 'safe'. I kept my share in a biscuit tin.'

The cash was tipped on to the table. An hour later they had finished counting. There was £17,301 and 10 shillings.

'What shall we do with it?' asked Ben

'Go shopping!' *It's easier than it seems*, she thought.

And they did. The following day there were two 'errands'. The first to the driving test centre, the second to Evans' where she'd bought her Mini. Brimming with confidence, Helen booked Ben's driving test appointment for three weeks ahead. Then at the garage Ben took a shine to an MGB sports car. The salesman remembered Helen and he was quite prepared for what he took to be her preferred method of doing business. She paid for the car in full, in cash, with instructions to register it in Ben's name, tax and insure it and have it ready for collection in three weeks' time. With at least £16,000 remaining in the box, Helen decreed that the contents of the box were at any time to be deemed 'housekeeping' money or petty cash. Having said so, the box was subsequently placed in a kitchen cupboard.

When Ben gave Tina the news of his new car, she was probably more excited than he was. Anyway, the pair of them were level-headed people and they both realised how important the next few months were. Ben's diploma exam, and perhaps a concert performance, and with Mock A-level exams to prepare for. Tina was equally busy, finishing off some sculptures for an exhibition she was mounting and her own A-level preparation. They both had the distraction of their eighteenth birthdays to look forward to as well. Not that either Ben or Tina were aware, but Albert and Dennis had plans afoot and were organising a surprise joint birthday party for them.

Chapter Fifty-One

Detective Inspector Mosely was sitting at his desk. Opposite him sat Detective Constable Cartwright. They were taking stock of where they'd got to in the case of 'the body in the lock' as it had become known. According to the pathologist's report, as far as she could be certain, they knew that the cause of death was a gunshot to the head. They knew that the body, thought to be that of a Ronald Nicholls, had been disposed of in the lock Number 25. And from the state of decomposition it was estimated that the murder occurred between fifteen and twenty years ago. Cartwright had been back through the records and discovered that during that time there had only been three missing persons reported that hadn't been found. The body in the lock was definitely not one of them but Helen Blake was or had been. They had a possible murder weapon; a WWII German Luger. Forensics had been unable to establish beyond reasonable doubt that it was the murder weapon. They had a suspect; a Duncan McClean, aka 'Jock' of no fixed abode but thought to have been living on a narrowboat, the *Emily Rose*. Jock seemed to have disappeared off the planet or into thin air. It was all very depressing for DI Mosely. In spite of the information they had accumulated so far the case was far from being solved.

Cartwright had more information.

'Jock had a known associate; Kenneth Blake but he was found dead almost two years ago, coincidently also in lock Number 25.'

'What?' he exploded. The inspector didn't like coincidences!

'The coroner recorded 'misadventure' but was it? I'm not so sure. Could Jock have bumped Blake off as well? Quite likely I'd say. MO's about the same.'

'Quite likely you say Cartwright? I think we need to have a word with Blake's family.' Mosely decided.

'His parents are still with us and I think there's a wife and son but they were separated from what I can make out,' Cartwright reported. The inspector dispatched his constable to see what he might discover from members of the family.

After two days Mosely was sitting at his desk. Cartwright was sitting opposite. Cartwright referred to his notebook.

'I started with the parents. Albert and Mabel both respectable pensioners. Two other siblings neither of which have lived in the area for years. Albert is as mystified as we are about the coroner's verdict but wouldn't want to pursue it. Apparently Ken's marriage didn't last long. He left her up the duff and went back to join his old regiment in Scotland. His daughter-in-law, Helen, had the baby and then buggered off but he couldn't give me any details. She was reported missing. Ken came back after about three years and he brought the boy up, Ben, in a council house of the Brookside estate. After Ken's death the son, Ben, lived with his grandparents. Seems it was the son who discovered his dad's body in the lock.'

Moseley appeared to be singularly unimpressed by anything Cartwright had reported thus far.

'Is that all you've got?'

'Oh no sir, there's more.'

'Go on then, get on with it man!' demanded Mosely impatiently.

'You won't like this bit sir because I know how you feel about coincidences. When they were first married shortly after the war, they lived at the same address as two of the missing persons who were reported eighteen years ago.'

'Oh no, don't tell me, they're in the bloody canal somewhere as well.'

'No sir they still haven't been found. That's a cold case now. Anyway Helen, and as I've said, she was the third missing person reported, the wife, she returned from wherever she'd been about the time of Ken's funeral and the boy Ben has now moved in with her. She's got a place in Burton Overy and doing very nicely by all accounts; made quite a lot of money from some investments, war bonds, apparently. The boy's at grammar school doing A-levels – a very talented pianist I'm told.'

'Is that it then? You've spent two days investigating this bloody mess and this is all you've come up with? You'll never make sergeant, Cartwright. Go on get out!' Inspector Mosely was less than impressed, and clearly having a bad day. As for the hapless Cartwright, he thought he'd done rather well.

Mosely knocked on the door or his superior's office, Detective Chief Inspector Rees. The DCI was treated to a full and detailed account of the 'body in the lock' case. In conclusion, Mosely suggested that it would be a waste of time pursuing it any further.

'No one's chasing us for results, nothing's missing, nobody's complaining, can we consign this one to the cold cases cabinet, sir?'

The DCI looked directly at Mosely and ruminated for half a minute, then agreed.

'Yes, I think you're probably right. File it!'

A week or so before the birthday party Helen called to see Albert ostensibly to check on the party arrangements. What she really wanted to check on was whether Albert had received a visit from the police, and if so, what had transpired. She was mightily relieved to hear that Albert had not divulged anything of an incriminating nature. For her part she told Albert what had transpired at her encounter with DC Cartwright. They both agreed that this was a situation where the whole truth would not serve anyone's interests, and honesty was certainly not the best policy. Even so, discretion would by necessity have to be their byword. The less said the better.

Chapter Fifty-Two

At the driving test centre, Helen and Tina sat nervously in the waiting room. Ben had been gone for almost half-an-hour and they were expecting him back at any moment. And then there he was. The expression on his face said so much more than he could have put into words right at that instant. Off they went to collect his birthday present.

They parked the Mini and all piled excitedly into the showroom. They were greeted immediately by the salesman turned showman. He took then over to a car shrouded beneath a red silk sheet. With a flamboyant flourish, the salesman whipped the sheet away to reveal the ravishingly radiant red MGB convertible. After the salesman had demonstrated the controls and various other features, not least of which was the manner in which the roof was lowered and raised and how the tonneau cover fitted, Ben couldn't wait to get behind the wheel. The salesman made a big show of opening the passenger door for Tina, handing her the folder of documentation with a gracious bow. As tempting as it might have been, it just wasn't 'roof-down' weather. Helen looked on, getting as much enjoyment from the expressions on the faces of Ben and Tina as they themselves were getting from being in the car.

'Tell you what, Ben,' Helen teased, 'I'll have this one, you can have the Mini!'

On the eve of the birthday party, Ben, Tina, Jamie and Diane all met in the Old Greyhound. Diane had the night off but even so George was continuously asking her to serve. She had certainly proved her worth behind the bar. Custom had never been so good. She was a proficient barmaid too! Whilst the girls had gone to the toilet, Jamie slipped Ben a piece of paper.

'Names and addresses of bullion dealers, thought it might be of interest,' he said with a wink. 'You'll also be pleased to hear that the police have closed their investigation of the body in the lock case. Mosely told my dad at his Masonic meeting last night.'

'What, they've solved it?'

'No, just not pursuing it any further.'

'Fantastic!' This was exactly the sort of deliverance he wanted; a better birthday gift even than the car. His mum would be absolutely ecstatic. He knew that she had been worrying herself sick since the police had been round asking questions.

'Jamie, that is indeed tremendous news. Terrific! How much lager do you reckon you can drink?'

Ben and Tina had gone out for a drive at Helen's suggestion. When they returned it was to a rousing chorus of 'Happy Birthday'. Tucked away behind the piano was Mr Sims and everywhere were Ben and Tina's friends and relatives. The house was packed. Some people knew each other and some didn't but it wouldn't be long before they did. Cards were piled up on the sideboard awaiting opening and there were several gifts too. Helen assisted by Diane, was keeping everyone's glass topped up, and laid out in the kitchen was a buffet of wedding reception proportions.

Ben and Tina managed to steal a private moment to themselves.

'This is the best birthday I've ever had,' Ben admitted.

'Me too,' whispered Tina.

Albert was tapping a spoon on the side of his glass and everyone's attention was drawn to what was surely going to be an important announcement.

'I have a birthday gift here for Ben.' He went on the explain for the benefit of those who didn't know, and as a reminder for those that did how Ben's formative years had been challenging; and how the challenge had culminated in the discovery of his dad's body in lock 25. The room was hushed with everyone hanging on Albert's every word. He described how Ben's ambition to become a pianist had almost been shattered, how his friendship with Tina had aided his rehabilitation, and how 'finding' his mother after so many years was a transport of delight that had delivered good fortune and prosperity to the whole family.

'Even though his mother went AWOL,' there were some giggles, 'she never forgot about her son. She remembered every birthday and now, on his eighteenth, I can hand over this gift from his mother.' Helen and Mabel both had their hankies out as Albert presented Ben with his savings account passbook. Ben took a sneaky peak inside. The total amount took his breath away. He'd learned to expect the unexpected, but...!

'Friends, relations, I give you Ben and Helen!' The toast resounded around the room. Mr Sims struck up with 'For He's a Jolly Good Fellow' which finished with a round of applause. Dennis stepped forward. A renewed silence prevailed.

'I don't know whether she's asked him yet, or whether she's waiting for the 29th February but at the risk of embarrassing them both we look forward to welcoming Ben into our family.' There was much cheering led by Jamie. Ben gave Tina a look which conveyed more than words; perhaps as well, given the noise. Ben simply mouthed, 'I love you!'

In spite of and despite all the hardships and difficulties, brushes with the law and living on the dark side, everything had turned out well. The weight on Helen's mind from her years as a profligate lost soul was becoming less of a burden although the voice of her conscience still reproached her from time to time. However the Blake family was now worth a fortune. Their financial security for the future was assured. Was not this in itself surely some form of atonement? Helen rarely thought of Ken, although she had kept the wedding photograph album. Yes, she had loved him but notwithstanding everything, had he deserved such an end? And Jock? Vanished down a black hole. Had he got away with murder? Seems he had. Or had he?

Her mind slipped back to that passage in a book she'd read or heard once-upon-a-time somewhere.

When you perform any task, it is easier than it seems in anticipation or even in retrospect because the different problems offer themselves little by little and in simplified form until no major and complex remains.

One day after school, on their way to the library Tina asked,

'How much was in your bank book?'

'A small fortune. Mum had been sending me £100 money order every birthday and grandad had opened the account for me and was paying it in. With interest, there's £2107 and some shillings and pence in there. Perhaps as well as it seems I'm engaged to be married.'

The End

Lightning Source UK Ltd.
Milton Keynes UK
UKHW020750291222
414571UK00015B/669